D1548507

The Girl From Farris's

The Girl
From Farris's

Edgar Rice Burroughs

WILDSIDE PRESS
Doylestown, Pennsylvania

The Girl From Farris's by Edgar Rice Burroughs, as originally published in *All-Story Weekly Magazine,* Frank A. Munsey Company, 1916.

The Girl From Farris's

A publication of

WILDSIDE PRESS

P.O. Box 301
Holicong, PA 18928-0301

www.wildsidepress.com

Introduction:

Master of Our Imagination

*I*f there is such a thing as a "collective subconscious" as proposed by Jung, then Edgar Rice Burroughs leapt into it and never left in 1917 when *Tarzan of the Apes* was published in England, and Burroughs's first Mars book found readers. That was the year before the end of the "Great War," a year of great trouble, and the aftermath of the terrible Influenza epidemic. Millions died in Europe and around the world, soldiers within the trenches, and civilians due to disease, starvation, and economic upheaval.

Imagine the Lord of Greystoke, raised in the Jungle. A man of honor, courage, and uncompromising principles, who knew nothing of Continental politics, Bolshevism, or anarchists with knives, guns and bombs. Imagine, too, a Mars of wonder, with great lords, Princesses, barbarians, and wondrous new inventions. And imagine them coming into a world of trouble and strife. Dreams do serve a purpose; and Edgar Rice Burroughs was nothing if not a great and powerful dreamer.

Burroughs's aficionados note that during his life-time, his work "failed to gather critical acclaim, yet influenced a generation." Like so many beloved writers, Burroughs followed the well-known path to story-telling success. Burroughs got a start in writing after some failed attempts at being a salesman, railroad policeman, and other professions; according to official biographies, he even had to pawn his wife's jewelry to make ends meet. He daydreamed and read pulp magazines, and one day decided that he could write a better pulp story than the ones he knew, and submitted his first tale to the *All-Story Magazine* at age 35, using the pseudonym "Normal Bean," believing that the story was so far-out and fantastic that no one would be interested. He shouldn't have worried. From that time forward, readers were hooked.

What can you say about a writer who created Tarzan of the Apes, John Carter of Mars, and David Innes of Pellucidar? A writer who took readers — for the first time, and for many, the times that they imagine and dream and remember always — to the African jungles, to the plains and canals of Mars, and to the magical world of Pellucidar? Worlds within our own, far more wondrous than any ever imagined before — Barsoom! Ray Bradbury fully acknowledges his debt to Edgar Rice Burroughs, and in this beautiful, childlike, dreaming bard's words can we see the reflection of Burroughs's dreams today. In truth, nearly every fantasy or science fiction writer, and certainly filmmakers, have drunk from the well of Edgar Rice Burroughs, and drunk deeply.

Ray Bradbury never spoke more movingly than at the Nebula Awards in 2001 in Beverly Hills, California. There is something of magic in him, just as there is something of complete wonder and magic in Edgar

Rice Burroughs. Ray Bradbury spoke, as he often does, of the importance of remaining a child, and this is true: there is something of the child in almost every great writer. Do you remember when you were young? How it seemed that if you only wished hard enough and thought hard enough and dreamed long enough, the magic might become real? Toys were not merely playthings, they were real, real friends, real companions, real comrades. And that boy in the jungle that every child knows, swinging from the trees, he can really talk to the lions and the elephants and the crocodiles and to "Cheetah." Tarzan can even talk to Jane. Now, if that's not magic, what is?

No one much compliments Burroughs on his prose, but here is how he introduces John Carter in *A Princess of Mars*: "I am a very old man; how old I do not know. Possibly I am a hundred, possibly more; but I cannot tell because I have never aged as other men, nor do I remember any childhood. So far as I can recollect I have always been a man, a man of about thirty. I appear today as I did forty years and more ago, and yet I feel that I cannot go on living forever; that some day I shall die the real death from which there is no resurrection." Perhaps the suggestion of Carter's agelessness is what offends "critics," but — John Carter may have feared that he would die the "real death," but the truth is — he'll live forever.

Chieftains, Princesses, Adventurers, Barbarians. Lush jungles, garden worlds, and a world within the Earth itself. This is the imagination of a profound dreamer, full of rich images that have fueled more than fifty Tarzan movies and famous Tarzans from Johnny Weismuller and Buster Crabbe to Ron Ely and Christopher Lambert. Fritz Leiber and Philip Jose Farmer have written Tarzan-inspired novels. It doesn't matter how many NASA probes return from Mars empty-handed: dreamers everywhere know that somewhere, sometime, somehow, Barsoom is real.

At the very Nebula Award ceremony where Ray Bradbury spoke, Philip Jose Farmer was named one of science fiction's "Grand Masters." Farmer came up with the idea that there is some kind of vast genetic "family" of heroes and adventurers, all related, and among these are Tarzan, John Carter, and other beloved Burroughs characters. This all sounds quite insane, but how else to explain this extraordinary combination of heroism, strength, and character?

Just like 1917, we are in a world whose moorings have come loose, a world filled with change, fear, and horrific, cataclysmic events. Perhaps these stories of Edgar Rice Burroughs, filled with wonder, adventure, miracles, heroes and villains as they are, fit the same need today as they did during that long-ago time. A distant jungle, to ponder about and imagine, a hero swinging to the rescue, calling nature itself to his aid. A man of adventure, beyond age and limitations, traversing the magical, mystical land of Mars. Pellucidar, whose very name conjures up images of beauty, mystery and wonder.

We are told that to grow up, we must put aside childish things; but what child ever went to war? What child ever flew a plane into a building which was itself a miracle, killing thousands, like the World Trade Towers? And who was ever too old to breathe in wonder at untold vistas beneath the earth, to think that a Princess of Mars was beautiful, to imagine the gardens of Mars and the deep, green jungles of Africa where a man grew to be a hero untouched by human hand?

Edgar Rice Burroughs himself told everyone that his only aim in writing was to "entertain." He wanted to take people's minds off their troubles for a few moments, give them laughter, pleasure and enjoyment.

Few, if any, have ever so entertained. Not just one, but many of his characters are as real to us as if they truly lived, breathed and walked. They are truly immortal: Tarzan will never die; John Carter still lives.

There is too much pain in this world, and too little wonder. Every so often, we receive gifts. And these, like Edgar Rice Burroughs, we ought not question, but rather, treasure.

Edgar Rice Burroughs created a full, rich panoply of characters and worlds of wonder. His work is timeless, like one of his invented worlds: *The Land That Time Forgot*. Edgar Rice Burroughs made pure, unadulterated magic.

— Amy Sterling Casil
February, 2002
Redlands, California

*F*ew authors, not even with the exception of Rudyard Kipling, have covered so wide a field in their fiction as has Mr. Burroughs. His maiden effort, which was published in the old *All-Story* in 1912, dealt with the adventures of an American who made a trip to Mars, and the things he saw there. Then he took a flier into the African jungle in his Tarzan tales, wrote some red-hot romance around a Central European kingdom, and turned his attention to a hero who was the brutalized product of a Chicago slum. Him he regenerated to such an extent that every reader we have, seemingly, voiced a raging demand for a sequel to *The Mucker* that should make that gentleman happy! And in this splendid novel, *The Girl from Farris's,* Mr. Burroughs has found yet another and really serious field, though he has given you as remarkable a heroine as you might expect. For the Girl was a member of "the oldest profession in the world," and the hero was foreman of the grand jury. Now go on with the story!

— THE EDITOR

(Robert H. Davis, editor of *All-Story* Magazine)

Chapter I

DOARTY MAKES A "PINCH"

*J*ust what Mr. Doarty was doing in the alley back of Farris's at two of a chill spring morning would have puzzled those citizens of Chicago who knew Mr. Doarty best.

To a casual observer it might have appeared that Mr. Doarty was doing nothing more remarkable than leaning against a telephone pole, which in itself might have been easily explained had Mr. Doarty not been so palpably sober; but there are no casual observers in the South Side levee at two in the morning — those who are in any condition to observe at all have the eyes of ferrets.

This was not the first of Mr. Doarty's nocturnal visits to the vicinage of Farris's. For almost a week he had haunted the neighborhood between midnight and dawn, for Mr. Doarty had determined to "get" Mr. Farris.

From the open doors of a corner saloon came bursts of bacchanal revelry — snatches of ribald song; hoarse laughter; the hysterical scream of a woman; but though this place, too, was Farris's and the closing hour long passed Mr. Doarty deigned not to notice so minor an infraction of the law.

Hadn't Lieutenant Barnut filed some ninety odd complaints against the saloon-keeper-alderman of the Eighteenth Ward for violation of this same ordinance, only to have them all pigeonholed in the city prosecutor's office? Hadn't he appeared in person before the September Grand Jury, and hadn't the state Attorney's office succeeded in bamboozling that August body into the belief that they had nothing whatsoever to do with the matter?

An anyhow, what was an aldermanic drag compared with that possessed by "Abe" Farris? No; Mr. Doarty, had you questioned him, would have assured you that he had not been born so recently as yesterday; that he was entirely dry behind the ears; and that if he "got" Mr. Farris at all he would get him good and plenty, for had he not only a week before, learning that Mr. Doarty was no longer in the good graces of his commanding officer, refused to acknowledge Mr. Doarty's right to certain little incidental emoluments upon which time-honored custom had placed the seal of lawful title?

In other words — Mr. Doarty's words — Abe Farris had not come across. Not only had he failed in this very necessary obligation, but he had added insult to injury by requesting Mr. Doarty to hie himself to the celestial nadir; and he had made his remarks in a loud, coarse tone of voice in the presence of a pock-marked barkeep who had it in for Mr. Doarty because of a certain sixty, weary, beerless days that the pock-marked one had spent at the Bridewell on Mr. Doarty's account.

But the most malign spleen becomes less virulent with age, and so it was that Mr. Doarty found his self-appointed task becoming irksome to a degree that threatened the stability of his Machiavellian resolve. Furthermore, he was becoming sleepy and thirsty.

"T' 'ell with 'im," sighed Mr. Doarty, sadly, as he removed his weight from the supporting pole to turn disconsolately toward the mouth of the alley.

At the third step he turned to cast a parting, venomous glance at the back of Farris's; but he took no fourth step toward the alley's mouth. Instead he dissolved, wraithlike, into the dense shadow between two barns, his eyes never leaving the back of the building that he had watched so assiduously and fruitlessly for the past several nights.

In the back of Farris's is a rickety fire escape — a mute, decaying witness to the lack of pull under which some former landlord labored. Toward this was Mr. Doarty's gaze directed, for dimly discernible upon it was something that moved — moved slowly and cautiously downward.

It required but a moment for Mr. Doarty's trained eye to transmit to his eager brain all that he required to know, for the moment at least, of the slow-moving shadow upon the shadowy ladder — the he darted across the alley toward the yard in the rear of Farris's.

A girl was descending the fire escape. How frightened she was she alone knew and that there must have been something very dreadful to escape in the building above her was apparent from the risk she took at each step upon that loose and rusted fabric of sagging iron.

She was clothed in a flowered kimono, over which she had drawn a black silk underskirt. Around her shoulders was an old red shawl, and she was shod only in bedroom slippers. Scarcely a suitable attire for street wear; but then people in the vicinity of Twenty-Fourth Street are not over particular about such matters; especially those who elect to leave their bed and board at two of a morning by way of a back fire escape.

At the first floor the ladder ended — a common and embarrassing habit of fire escape ladders, which are as likely as not to terminate twenty feet above a stone areaway, or a picket fence — but the stand pipe continued on to the ground. A stand pipe, flat against a brick wall, is not an easy thing for a young lady in a flowered kimono and little else to negotiate; but this was an unusual young lady, and great indeed must have been the stress of circumstance which urged her on, for she came down the stand pipe with the ease of a cat, and at the bottom, turned, horrified, to look into the face of Mr. Doarty.

With a little gasp of bewilderment she attempted to dodge past him, but a huge paw of a hand reached out and grasped her shoulder.

"Well dearie?" said Mr. Doarty.

"Cut it out," replied the girl, "and le'me loose. Who are you anyhow?"

For answer Mr. Doarty pulled back the lapel of his coat disclosing a shiny piece of metal pinned on his suspender.

"I ain't done nothing," said the girl.

"Of course you ain't," agreed Mr. Doarty. "Don't I know that real ladies always climb down fire escapes at two o'clock in the morning just to prove that they ain't done nothin'?"

"Goin' to pinch me?"

"Depends," replied the plain-clothes man. "What's the idea of this nocturnal get-away."

The girl hesitated.

"Give it to me straight," admonished her captor. "It'll go easier with you."

"I guess I might as well," she said. "You see I get a swell offer from the Beverly Club, and that fat schonacker," she gave a vindictive nod of her head toward the back of Farris's resort, "he gets it tipped off to him some way, and has all my clothes locked up so as I can't get away."

"He wouldn't let you out of his place, eh?" asked Mr. Doarty, half to himself.

"He said I owed him three hundred dollars for board and clothes."

"An' he was keepin' you a prisoner there against your will?" purred Mr. Doarty.

"Yes," said the girl.

Mr. Doarty grinned. This wasn't exactly the magnitude of the method he had hoped to "get" Mr. Farris; but it was better than nothing. The present Grand Jury was even now tussling with the vice problem. Hours of its valuable time were being taken up by reformers who knew all about the general conditions with which every adult citizen is familiar; but the tangible cases, backed by the sort of evidence that convicts, were remarkable only on account of there scarcity.

Something seemed always to seal the mouths of the principal witnesses the moment they entered the Grand Jury room; but here was a case where personal spite and desire for revenge might combine to make an excellent witness against the most notorious dive keeper in the city. It was worth trying for.

"Come along," said Mr. Doarty.

"Aw, don't. Please don't!" begged the girl. "I ain't done nothing, honest!"

"Sure you ain't," replied Mr. Doarty. "I'm only goin' to have you held as a witness against Farris. That'll get you even with him, and give you a chance to get out and take that swell job at the Beverly Club."

"They wouldn't have me if I peached on Farris, and you know it. Why, I couldn't get a job in a house in town if I done that."

"How would you like to be booked for manslaughter?" asked the plain clothes man.

"What you giving me!" laughed the girl. "Stow the kid."

"It ain't no kid," replied Mr. Doarty solemnly. "The police knows a lot about the guy that some one croaked up in Farris's in March, but we been layin' low for a certain person as is suspected of passin' him the drops. It gets tipped off to the inmates of Farris's, an' I bein' next, spots her as she is makin' her get-away. Are you hep?"

The young lady was hep — most assuredly who would not be hep to the very palpable threat contained in Mr. Doarty's pretty little fiction?

"An'," continued Doarty, "when Farris finds you been tryin' to duck he won't do nothin' to help you."

The girl had known of many who had gone to the pen on slighter evidence than this. She knew that the police had been searching for some one upon whom to fasten the murder of a well known business man who had not been murdered at all, but who had had the lack of foresight to succumb to an attack of acute endocarditis in the hallway of the Farris place.

The searching eyes of the plain-clothes man had not failed to detect the little shudder of horror that had been the visible reaction in the girl to the sudden recollections induced by mention of that unpleasant affair, and while he had no reason whatever to suspect her or another of any criminal responsibility for the man's death, yet he made a mental note of the effect his words had had upon her.

Had she not been an inmate of the house at the time the thing occurred? And was it not just possible that an excellent police case might be worked up about her later if the exigencies of the service demanded a brilliant police *coup* to distract the public's attention from some more important case in which they had blundered?

For a moment the girl was silent. How badly he had frightened her with his threat Mr. Doarty had not the faintest conception, nor, could he have guessed the pitiable beating of her heart, would he have been able to conjecture the real cause of her alarm. That the policeman would assume criminal guilt in her should she allow her perturbation to become too apparent she well knew, and so, for the moment of her silence, she struggled to regain mastery of herself. Nor was she unsuccessful.

"It wouldn't get you anything," she said, "to follow that lay, for the report of the coroner's physician shows that Mr. — that the man died of heart disease. But, cutting out all this foolishness, I'll swear a complaint against Farris if you want me to — if you thing that it will get you anything. Though, and you can take it from me who knows, it's more likely to get you a prairie beat out Brighton way — there's many a bull pullin' his box to-night out in the wilderness who thought that he could put one over on Abe Farris — and Farris is still doin' business at the old stand."

As they talked they had been walking toward the street, and now Doarty crossed over to the corner with the girl and pulled for the wagon.

"What did it stand you to forget the guy's name? he asked, after they had stood in silence for a time awaiting the wagon's tardy arrival.

"They offered me a hundred," she replied.

"An', of course, you didn't take it," he ventured, grinning.

The girl made no response.

"The newspapers sure suffered an awful shock when they found the old bloke was one of the biggest stockholders in two State Street department stores," continued Mr. Doarty reminiscently.

"They say his family routed the advertising manager of every paper in the city out of bed at one o'clock in the morning, and that three morning papers had to pull out the story after they had gone to press with it, and stick in a column obituary tellin' all about what he had done for his city and his fellow man, with a cut of his mug in place of the front page cartoon — gee! But it must be great to have a drag like that."

"Yes," said the girl in a faint voice.

Faintly in the distance a gong clanged.

"Them guys is sure takin' their time," observed Mr. Doarty.

A little crowd had gathered about the couple at the police-box, only mildly curious, for an arrest is no uncommon thing in that section of town; and when they discovered that no one had been cut up, or shot up, and that the prisoner was scandalously sober they ceased even to be mildly curious. By the time the wagon arrived the two were again alone.

At the station the girl signed a complaint against one Abe Farris, and was then locked up to insure her appearance in court the following morning.

Officer Doarty, warrant in hand, fairly burned the pavement back to Farris's. It had been many a month since he had made an arrest which gave him as sincere personal pleasure as this one. He routed Farris out of bed and hustled him into his clothes. This, he surmised, might be the sole satisfaction that he would derive, since the municipal court judge before whom the preliminary hearing would come later in the morning might, in all likelihood, discharge the defendant.

If the girl held out and proved a good witness there was a slight chance that Farris would be held to the Grand Jury, in which event he would derive a certain amount of unpleasant notoriety at a time when public opinion was aroused by the vice question, and the mayor in a most receptive mood for making political capital by revocation of a few saloon licenses.

All this would prove balm to Mr. Doarty's injured sensibilities.

Farris grumbled and threatened, but off to the station he went without even an opportunity to telephone for a bondsman. That he procured one an hour later was no fault of Mr. Doarty, who employed his most persuasive English in an endeavor to convince the sergeant that Mr. Farris should be locked up forthwith, and given no access to a telephone until daylight. But the sergeant had no particular grudge against Mr. Farris, while, on the other hand, he was possessed of a large family to whom his monthly pay check was an item of considerable importance. So to Mr. Farris, he was affable courtesy personified.

Thus it was that the defendant went free, while the injured one remained behind prison bars.

Farris's first act was to obtain permission to see the girl who had sworn to the complaint against him. As he approached her cell he assumed a jocular suavity that he was far from feeling.

"What you doin' here, Maggie?" he asked, by way of an opening.

"Ask Doarty."

"Didn't you know that you'd get the worst of it if you went to buckin' me?" queried Farris.

"I didn't want to do it," replied the girl; " though that's not sayin' that some one hadn't ought to do it to you good an' proper — you got it comin' to you, all right."

"It won't get you nothin', Maggie."

"Maybe it'll get me my clothes — that's all I want."

"Why didn't you say so in the first place, then, and not go stirrin' up a lot of hell this way?" asked Farris in an injured tone. "Ain't I always been on the square with you?"

"Sure! You been as straight as a corkscrew with me."

"Didn't I keep the bulls from guessin' that you was the only girl in the place that had any real reason for wantin' to croak old — the old guy?" continued Mr. Farris, ignoring the reverse English on the girl's last statement.

A little shiver ran through the girl at mention of the tragedy that was still fresh in her memory — her own life tragedy in which the death of the old man in the hallway at Farris's had been but a minor incident.

"What you goin' to tell the judge?" asked Farris after a moment's pause.

"The truth — that you kept me there against my will by locking my clothes up where I couldn't get 'em," she replied.

"I was only kiddin — you could 'a' had 'em any old time. Anyways, there wasn't no call for your doin' this."

"You got a funny way of kiddin'; but even at that, I didn't have any idea of peachin' on you — he made me," said the girl.

"Who? Doarty?"

The girl nodded. "Sure — who else? He's got it in for you."

Farris turned away much relieved, and an hour later a colored man delivered a package at the station for Maggie Lynch. It contained the girl's clothes, and an envelope in which were five germ-laden but perfectly good, ten-dollar bills.

The matron smiled as she opened the envelope.

"Some fox," she said.

"Some fox, is right," replied the girl.

Chapter II

AND WIRES ARE PULLED

*T*he Rev. Theodore Pursen sat at breakfast. With his right hand he dallied with iced cantaloupe. The season was young for *cucumis melo*; but who would desire a lean shepherd for a fat flock? Certainly not the Rev. Theodore Pursen. A slender, well-manicured left hand supported an early edition of the "Monarch of the Mornings," a sheet which quite made up in volume of sound and in color for any lack of similarity in other respects to the lion of poetry and romance.

On the table in his study were the two morning papers which the Rev. Pursen read and quoted in public — the Monarch was for the privacy of his breakfast table.

Across from the divine sat his young assistant, who shared the far more than comfortable bachelor apartments of his superior.

The Rev. Pursen laid down the paper with a sigh.

"Ah me," he said.

His assistant looked up in polite interrogation.

"This is, indeed, an ungrateful world," continued Mr. Pursen, scooping a delicious mouthful from the melon's heart.

"Here is an interview with an assistant State attorney in which he mentions impractical reformers seeking free advertising and cheap notoriety. In view of the talk I had with him yesterday I cannot but believe that he refers directly to me

"It is a sad commentary upon the moral perspective of the type of rising young men of to-day, which this person so truly represents, that ulterior motives should be ascribed to every noble and unselfish act. To what, indeed, are we coming?"

"Yes," agreed the assistant, "whither are we drifting?"

"But was it not ever thus? Have not we of the cloth been ever martyrs to the cause of truth and righteousness?"

"Too true," sighed the assistant, "we have, indeed."

"Yet, on the other hand," continued Mr. Pursen, "there is an occasional note of encouragement that makes the fighting of the battle worth while."

"For example?" suggested the assistant.

Mr. Pursen turned again to the "Monarch of the Mornings."

"Here is a quarter of a column devoted to an interview with me on the result of my investigation of conditions in supposedly respectable residence districts. The article has been given much greater prominence than that accorded to the misleading statements of the assistant State attorney. I am sure that thousands of people in this great city are even this minute reading this noticeable heading — let us hope that it will bear fruit, however much one may decry the unpleasant notoriety entailed."

Mr. Pursen held up the newspaper toward his assistant, who read, in type half an inch high:

PURSEN PILLORIES POLICE

"The ointment surrounding the fly, as it were," suggested the assistant.

Mr. Pursen looked quickly at the young man, but discovering no sign of levity in his expression, handed the paper across the table to him and resumed his attack upon the cantaloupe. A moment later the telephone-bell sounded from the extension at Mr. Pursen's elbow.

"Yes?" inquired Mr. Pursen.

"Hello. Dr. Pursen?"

"Yes."

"This is Doarty."

"Oh, yes; good morning, officer," greeted Mr. Pursen.

Mr. Doarty came right to the point. He knew when to beat about the bush and when not to.

"You been tryin' to close up Farris's place for six months; but you ain't never been able to get the goods on him. I got 'em for you, now."

"Good," exclaimed Mr. Pursen. " Tell me about it."

Mr. Doarty unburdened himself.

"The girl will be in court this morning to appear against Farris," he concluded. "You'd better get to her quick, before they do, and stick until she's called. She'll need bolstering."

"I'll come down right away," replied Mr. Pursen. "Good-by, and thank you."

"And say," said Doarty, "you can give it out that you tipped me off to the whole thing — I'd just as soon not appear in it any more than I can help."

"Just so," replied Mr. Pursen, and hung up the receiver.

As he turned back his assistant eyed him questioningly.

"My friend Mr. Doarty has started something which be is experiencing difficulty in terminating," guessed Mr. Pursen shrewdly.

At a quarter before ten the clergyman entered the court-room. He had no difficulty in locating the girl he sought, though the room was well filled with witnesses, friends, and relatives of the various prisoners who were to have their preliminary hearings, and the idle curious.

"I am the Rev. Mr. Pursen," he said with smiling lips as he took her hand.

The girl looked him squarely in the eyes.

"I come as a friend," continued Mr. Pursen. "I wish to help you. Tell me your story and we will see what can be done."

There were three young men with the clergyman. They had met him, by appointment, at the entrance to the courtroom. The girl eyed them.

"Reporters?" she asked.

"Representatives of the three largest papers," replied Mr. Pursen. "You will be quite famous by to-morrow morning," be added playfully.

When Mr. Pursen had introduced himself a great hope had sprung momentarily into the girl's heart — a longing that three months at Farris's had all but stifled. Vain regrets seldom annoyed her now. She had attained a degree of stoicism that three months earlier would have seemed impossible; but with contact with one from that other world which circumstances had forbidden her ever again to hope to enter — with the voicing of a kind word — with the play of a smile that was neither carnal nor condescending came a sudden welling of the desire she had thought quite dead — the desire to put behind her forever the life that she had been living.

For an instant a little girl had looked into the eyes of the Rev. Mr. Pursen, prepared to do and be whatever Mr. Pursen, out of the fullness of brotherly love, should counsel and guide her to do and be; but Mr. Pursen saw only a woman of the town, and to such were his words addressed with an argument which he imagined would appeal strongly to her kind. And it was a woman of the town who answered him with a hard laugh.

"Nothing doing," she said.

Mr. Pursen was surprised. He was pained. He had come to her as a friend in need. He had offered to help her, and she would not even confide in him.

"I had hoped that you might wish to lead a better life," he said, "and I came prepared to offer you every assistance in securing a position where you might earn a respectable living. I can find a home for you until such a position is forthcoming. Can you not see the horrors of the life you have chosen? Can you not realize the awful depths of degradation to which you have come, and the still blacker abyss that yawns before you if you continue along the downward path? Your beauty will fade quickly — its lifeblood sapped by the gnawing canker of vice and shame, and then what will the world hold for you? Naught but a few horrible years of premature and hideous old age."

"And the way to start a new and better life," replied the girl in a level voice, "is to advertise my shame upon the front pages of three great daily newspapers — that's your idea, eh?"

Mr. Pursen flushed, very faintly.

"You misunderstand me entirely," he said. "I abhor as much as any human being can the necessity which compels so much publicity in these matters; but it is for the greatest good of the greatest numbers that I labor — that all of us should labor. If the public does not know of the terrible conditions which prevail under their very noses, how can we expect it to rouse itself and take action against these conditions?

"No great reform is ever accomplished except upon the clamorous demand of the people. The police — in fact all city officials — know of these conditions; but they will do nothing until they are forced to do it. Only the people who elect them and whose money pays them can force them. We must keep the horrors of the underworld constantly before the voters and tax-payers until they rise and demand that the festering sore in the very heart of their magnificent city be cured forever.

"What are my personal feelings, or yours, compared with the great good to the whole community that will result from the successful fruition of the hopes of those of us who are fighting this great battle against the devil and his minions? You should rather joyfully embrace this opportunity to cast off the bonds of hell, and by enlisting with the legion of righteousness atone for all your sinful past by a self-sacrificing act in the interest of your fellow man."

The girl laughed, a rather unpleasant, mirthless laugh.

"My 'fellow man'!" She mimicked the preacher's oratorical style. "It was my fellow man who made me what I am; it was my fellow man who has kept me so! it is my fellow man who wished me to blazon my degradation to the world as a price for aid."

As she spoke, the vernacular of the underworld with its coarse slang and vile English slipped from her speech like a shabby disguise that has been discarded, and she spoke again as she had spoken in her other life, before constant association with beasts and criminals had left their mark upon her speech as upon her mind and morals; but as the first flush of indignation passed she slipped again into the now accustomed rut.

"To hell with you and your fellow men," she said. " Now beat it."

Mr. Pursen's dignity bad suffered a most severe shock. He glanced at the three young men. They were grinning openly. He realized the humiliating stories they would write for their respective papers. Not at all the kind of stories he had been picturing to himself, in which the Rev. Mr. Pursen would shine as a noble Christian reformer laboring for the salvation of the sinner and the uplift of the community. They would make horrid jokes of the occurrence, and people would laugh at the Rev. Mr. Pursen.

A stinging rebuke was upon his lips. He would make this woman realize the great gulf that lay between the Rev. Mr. Pursen and such as she. He would let her see the loathing with which a good man viewed her and her kind; but as he opened his mouth to speak, his better judgment came to his rescue. The woman would doubtless make a scene — her sort had a decided penchant for such things — she might even resort to physical violence.

In either event the resultant newspaper stories would be decidedly worse than the most glaring exaggerations which the three young men might concoct from the present unfortunate occurrence.

So the Rev. Mr. Pursen stifled his true emotions, and with a sorrowful shake of his head turned sadly from his thankless task; and, indeed, why should a shepherd waste his valuable time upon a worthless sheep that preferred to stay astray? It was evident that he had lost sight entirely of the greater good that would follow the conviction of Farris, for he had not even mentioned the case to the girl or attempted to encourage her to make the most of this opportunity to bring the man to justice.

Farris's case was called shortly after the clergyman left the court-room. The man had an array of witnesses present to swear that the girl had remained in his house of her own volition — that she could have left when she pleased; but the girl's story, coupled with the very evident fact that she was wholly indifferent as to the outcome of the case, resulted in the holding of Farris to the grand jury.

It was what the resort-keeper had anticipated, and as he was again released on bail he lost no time in seeking out the head of a certain great real-estate firm and laying before him a brief outline of the terrible wrong that was being contemplated against Mr. Farris, and, incidentally, against present real-estate rental values in the district where Mr. Farris held forth.

"You see," said Mr. Farris, "there ain't nothin' to this thing, anyway. It's just a case of the girl bein' sore on me because I had fired her, so she cooks up this story and gets me pinched. It's a shame, and me giving her a good home and a swell job when she didn't know nobody in the burg.

"It's too bad," and Mr. Farris heaved an oily sigh. "It's too damn bad when you think of what it'll mean to the property owners down there. Why, if the grand jury votes a true bill against me it'll start them fake reformers buzzin' around thick as flies in the whole district, and there won't be nothin' to it but a bunch of saloon licenses taken away by the mayor, and a string of houses closed up; and then where'll you be?

"Why, the best you can do for years'll be to rent them places to furriners at six and eight dollars a month, and just look at the swell rents you're gettin' for 'em now. Yes, sir! Somethin's got to be done in the interests of property values down there, for after we go you couldn't get decent people to live in the neighborhood if you paid 'em, to say nothin' of gettin' rent from 'em

— why, they can't even use 'em for business purposes!
Customers wouldn't dare come into the neighborhood
for fear some one would see them, and straight girls
wouldn't work in no such locality.

"If I was you I'd get busy. See your principals this
mornin', and get 'em to put it up straight to the State
attorney that it ain't in the interests of public morality
to push this reform game no further. Why, look what
it'll do — close up the red-light district, an' you'll have
them girls scattered all through the residence districts,
wherever they can rent a little flat; maybe right next
door to you an' your family. And then look at what
that'll do to property everywhere. It won't be only the
old levee values that'll slump, but here and there
through the residence districts North, South, and West
them girls'll get in and put whole blocks on the blink.

"Well, I guess you know as much about it as I do,
anyway; so I'll blow along. I got to see my alderman,
and if I had the front that you and your principals can
put up I'd see" — and here Mr. Farris leaned forward
and whispered a name into the real-estate agent's ear.
"He can put the kibosh on this whole reform game if
he wants to; and take it from me, there ain't nobody
that can't be made to want to do anything on earth if
you can find the way to get 'em where they live," and
Mr. Farris slapped his right-hand trouser-pocket until
the coins therein rang merrily.

The real-estate agent pursed his lips and shook his
head.

"You cannot reach that man in any such way as that,"
he said.

Mr. Farris, rising, laughed. "Oh splash," he said, and
started for the door. "Well, do what you can at your
end, and I'll work from the bottom up: and say, don't
forget that if you sugar-coat it, the best of 'em will grab
for it."

Then he went and had a talk with his alderman, who, in turn, saw some one else, who saw some one else, who saw another party; and the real-estate agent saw several of his principals, and at luncheon he talked with many of his colleagues, who hastened forthwith to confer with the big men whose property they handled.

In a day or two there began to filter into the State attorney's office by mail, by phone, and by personal call a continuous stream of requests that he move with extreme caution in the fight against vice which the reformers were urging him to initiate.

The arguments all were similar. They harped upon the danger of scattering the vicious element through-out the city — they were pleas for the safety of the wives and daughters of the petitioners.

"Abolish the red light district," said one, "and the criminals and degenerates of the underworld will hunt our wives and daughters as the wolves of the North woods hunt their prey — there will be no safety for them upon the streets nor within their own homes. Banish the women of the levee, and a state of anarchy and rapine will follow. For the sake of the good women of the city I pray that you will stand firm against the fallacious arguments of paid reformers and notoriety seekers."

No one mentioned property values — the pill had been properly coated. The State attorney smiled. Mentally he had been roughly estimating the political influence of each petitioner. When an editorial appeared in one of the leading dailies under the caption, "Go Slow, Mr. State Attorney," in which all these arguments were rehashed and the suggestion made that another commission be appointed to investigate and recommend a solution of the vice problem, he laughed aloud, for did he not know that the uncles and aunts and sisters-in-law of that great paper owned nearly a third of the real estate in the segregated district?

But the State attorney knew that no man knew what would be the result of the adoption of the drastic suggestions of the reformers, so it was an easy matter for him to justify himself to himself when he waged his bitter war of words against vice, and gave private instructions to his assistants in the safety and seclusion of his own office — instructions that did not always exactly harmonize with the noble sentiments enunciated in the typewritten "statements" passed out impartially to the representatives of the press for publication.

The State attorney was far from being a corrupt man; but the vice problem had been the plaything of reformers and politicians for years; it was as old as the sexes; it never had been solved, and the chances were that it never would be. If he had spoken his mind he would probably have admitted that he was afraid of it, entirely from sociological reasons, and apart from its political aspect.

But the State attorney was in no position to speak his true mind on many subjects — he hoped, some day, to run for Governor.

And so it was that he called an assistant to his office and poured words of wisdom into his attentive ear.

"And what sort of a bunch have you got this month?" he concluded.

"Oh, just about as usual. A couple of bank presidents, some retired capitalists, several department managers, and one farmer. They're new now, but by the time that case reaches us they'll be tired of the grind and ready to jump through whenever I tell 'em to."

Thus spake the young assistant State attorney of the ancient and honorable grand jury.

Chapter III

THE GRAND JURY

*T*wo weeks had elapsed since Mr. Farris had been held for the grand jury. He had been at liberty on bail. The girl, against whom there had been no charge, had been held, virtually a prisoner, in a home for erring women that she might be available as a witness when needed.

The grand jury was returning after lunch for the afternoon session. Something they had done the previous day had aroused the assistant State attorney's ire, so that he had felt justified in punishing their foolish temerity with two calls that day instead of one.

A little group had gathered in the front of the jury-room. They were discussing the cases passed, and speculating upon those to come. One and all were wearied with the monotony of the duty the State had imposed upon them.

"And the worst of it is," said one of the younger members of the panel, "it's all so utterly futile. When I was summoned as a grand juror I had a kind of feeling that the State had placed a great responsibility upon my shoulders, that she had honored me above other men, and placed me in a position where I might help to accomplish something really worth while for my fellow man."

One of the bank presidents laughed.

"And the reality you find to be quite different, eh?"

"Quite. I hear only one side of a great string of sordid, revolting stories, and I hear nothing more than the assistant State attorney wishes me to hear. There are momentous questions stirring the people of the city, but when we suggest that we should investigate the conditions underlying them we are told that we are not an investigating body — that those questions are none of our business unless they are brought to our attention through the regular channel of the State attorney's office. We are told that the judge who charged us to investigate these very conditions had never charged a grand jury before, and while doubtless he meant well he didn't know what he was talking about."

"I understand," said another juror, "that we will get our chance at the vice problem to-day 'through the regular channel' — the Abe Farris case is on the docket for this afternoon."

"And what will we do?" asked the young man. " We'll listen to answers to such questions as the assistant State attorney sees fit to ask, and if we start asking embarrassing questions he'll have the sergeant-at-arms hustle the witness out of the jury-room. Then we'll hem and haw, and end up by doing whatever the assistant State attorney wants us to do. We've done it on every important case — you watch."

"You are quite right, sir," spoke up a retired capitalist. "In theory the grand jury system is the bulwark of our liberty — it was, in fact, when it was instituted in the twelfth or thirteenth century, at a time when there were several hundred crimes punishable by death; but now that there are only two, murder and treason; it is a useless and wasteful relic of a dead past.

"The court that is competent to hold men to the grand jury is much more competent to indict them than is the grand jury itself. In fact, in cases where the punishment is less than death the court that now entertains the preliminary hearing might, to much better advantage to both the accused and public, pass sentence at once. It hears both sides, but all that it can do is discharge the prisoner or hold him for the grand jury. After this there is the expense of holding the prisoner in jail until his case comes to us, and then all the expensive paraphernalia of a grand jury is required to thresh over only one side of what has already been thoroughly heard before a trained and competent jurist. If we vote a true bill a third expensive trial is necessitated."

"Personally," said Ogden Secor, the foreman of the jury, "the whole thing strikes me as a farce. The grand jury, while not quite the tool of the State attorney's office, is considered by them a more or less harmless impediment to the transaction of the business of their office — a burden to be borne, but lightened in the most expeditious manner.

"I, as foreman, am a dummy; the secretary is a dummy; the sergeant-at-arms is a dummy. We look to the assistant State attorney for direction in our every move. We come from businesses in which we have never, in all probability, come in contact with criminal law, and we are expected to grasp the machinery of our new duties on a moment's notice.

"Were it purely a matter of justice to be dispensed, I have no doubt but that we might do quite as well as any court; but we are up against a very different thing from justice — at every hand we are trammeled by law."

The assistant State attorney entered the room.

"Sorry to have been late, gentlemen," he said. "Call the next case, Mr. Sergeant-at-arms," and the routine of the jury-room commenced half an hour after the appointed time, although a quorum of the grand jury had been present for thirty-five minutes.

The last case of the afternoon call was that against Abe Farris. There were only two witnesses — Officer Doarty and the girl, Maggie Lynch. Doarty had suffered a remarkable change of heart since the evening he stood in the alley back of Farris's. He was chastened in spirit. His recollection of the affair was vague. After the assistant State attorney had ceased questioning him several of the jurors asked additional information.

"What sort of person is the complaining witness, officer?" asked the banker.

Mr. Doarty looked about and grinned sheepishly. He would not have been at a loss for a word to describe her had a fellow policeman asked him this question, but this august body of dignified business men seemed to call for a special brand of denatured diction in the description of a spade.

"Oh," he said finally, "she's just like the rest of 'em down there — she's on the town."

"Would you believe her story?" asked the banker.

Doarty grinned and shrugged. "Hard to say," he replied.

"In your opinion, officer," asked the assistant State attorney, "have you any case against Farris? Could we get a conviction?"

"No, I don't think you could," answered the policeman. It was the question he had been awaiting.

"That's all, officer," said the assistant State attorney. "Just a moment, Mr. Sergeant-at-arms, before you call another witness."

"A moment, please, officer; I want to ask another question before you go," spoke up one of the jurymen.

The assistant State attorney sighed and looked bored. He had found this the most effective means of silencing jurymen.

"As I understand it, you worked this case up, am I right?" asked the juryman.

"Yes, sir."

"If you had enough evidence three weeks ago to warrant the arrest of Farris, why haven't you got enough now to insure conviction?"

Doarty looked uncomfortable. He fingered his cap, and turned an appealing look toward the assistant State attorney. That functionary came to his rescue.

"You see, Mr. — a — Smith, pardon me for interrupting," he said, "the girl swore out a warrant, and it was necessary to make the arrest. That's all, officer, you may go now."

"But," insisted Mr. Smith, "it was quite apparent from the newspaper account at the time that the girl was an unwilling complainant — that the police officer worked up the case."

In the mean time, Doarty, only too anxious to do so, had left the grand jury-room. The sergeant-at-arms stood with his hand upon the knob of the door looking questioningly at the assistant State attorney.

"You do not care to question any other witnesses, do you?" asked that young gentleman of the jury.

"What other witnesses are there?" asked Mr. Smith.

"Only the girl," replied the assistant State attorney; "but you can see from the officer's testimony that it is scarcely worth our while to hear from the girl. You might as well take a vote, Mr. Foreman," he concluded, turning toward Ogden Secor.

"All those in favor of a true bill raise their right hands," commanded Mr. Secor.

"Just a moment, Mr. Foreman," interrupted Mr. Smith.

The assistant State attorney scowled and sighed, then settled back in his chair in martyrlike resignation. Mr. Smith was a thorn in the flesh.

"It seems to me, Mr. Foreman," said Mr. Smith, "that until we have heard all the witnesses we are in no position to vote intelligently. I, for one, am in favor of calling in the girl."

"Yes," " Yes," came from several of the jurors.

The sergeant-at-arms looked toward the assistant State attorney for authority.

"Call the next witness," said Ogden Secor.

The sergeant-at-arms was surprised to receive a command from the foreman of the jury, but the assistant State attorney made no demur, so he opened the door.

"Next witness!" he called, and the grand jury clerk, whose office is just outside the grand jury-room, beckoned to a girl who sat in a chair in the far corner shielding her face with her arm from the glaring eyes of two press cameras. As she rose two flashlights exploded simultaneously. Then she hurried across the room and passed through the doorway into the presence of the grand jury.

Ogden Secor had had not the faintest curiosity regarding her. From earliest boyhood he had learned to shudder at the very thought of the hideous, painted creatures who plied their sickening vocation in a part of the town to which neither business, accident, nor inclination, had ever led him. For a city-bred man whose boyhood had been surrounded with every luxury and whose spending allowance had been practically unlimited, he was remarkably clean. His high ideals were still unsullied, and though a man's man mentally and physically, morally he was almost a prude.

It was with difficulty that he raised his eyes to the girl's face as he administered the oath, and it was with a distinct shock of surprised incredulity that he saw that she was neither painted nor hideous. Her brown eyes fell the moment that they met his — there was no slightest sign of boldness in them, and when she turned to face the jury as the assistant State attorney began questioning her her attitude was merely of quiet self-possession.

The young foreman could not reconcile the refinement of her appearance and the well-modulated voice with his preconceived ideas concerning her kind. He had been prepared for a sort of coarse, animal beauty, perhaps, and he had fully expected gaudy apparel and quantities of cheap jewelry; but instead he saw a demure, quietly dressed girl who might have stepped fresh from a convent. It was appalling to think that she had been an inmate of Farris's.

As she answered the often brutal questions of the assistant State attorney Ogden Secor watched her profile. He saw that the girl was actually suffering under the ordeal; and he had thought that she would welcome the notoriety and brazenly flaunt her shame in the faces of the jurymen!

And he saw, too, as he studied her face, that she was not merely ordinarily good-looking — hers was a face that would have been commented upon anywhere as exceptionally beautiful. He could not believe that the girl before him had voluntarily chosen the career she had been following.

The assistant State attorney had finished questioning her. He had brought out only the simple story she had told Doarty the night he had discovered her upon the fire-escape. It had not been a part of his plan to bring out much of anything bearing on the case. When he had finished Mr. Smith arose.

"How did you happen to be at Farris's place at all?" he asked. " Did you go there of your own volition?"

"Yes," replied the girl.

"You knew the life that you would have to lead there?"

" No; I did not know what kind of place it was."

"Tell us how you came there then," said Mr. Smith.

"I would rather not," she replied. "It has no bearing upon this case."

"Would you go back there if Farris would take you?" asked another jury-man.

"He will not take me."

"What do you intend doing?"

"I shall have to go to some other city where I am not known."

"And there you will continue the — ah — the same vocation?"

"What else is there for me?" she asked.

"There are many good men who would help you," said Mr. Smith. She shrugged, and for the first time Secor caught a note of hardness in her voice as she replied.

"There are no good men," she said.

There was a finality to her statement that put an end to further questioning.

Chapter IV

DECENCY

"THAT is all," said the assistant State attorney with a wave toward the door. The girl stepped down from the witness-stand. As she passed him a sudden impulse prompted Ogden Secor to stop her. He could not have explained why he did so, but before he realized it he had asked the girl to wait in the witness-room without until he came.

A great and sudden pity for her had welled within him at her last words: *"There are no good men."* To have spoken to such a woman as she would have seemed an utter impossibility to Ogden Secor a brief half-hour before, and now he had asked her to wait for him, and in his mind was a determination to help her — to save her from the hideous life she had chosen.

Immediately after he had spoken the words he regretted them. It was as though he had bound himself to personal contact with a leper. He paled a little at the thought of the ordeal which faced him; but he would go through with it, as to that he was determined, and if he could help the girl to a better life he would do so. Had he guessed the interpretation the girl put upon his request to speak with her outside the jury-room he would have flushed rather than paled. To her all men were hunters — all women quarry.

The jurors were discussing the wisdom of voting a true bill. All seemed to harbor not the slightest doubt that the girl had been held against her will in Farris's place. Had the vote been taken without discussion a true bill would have been the unanimous result; but with the discussion came the inevitable recourse to the superior legal judgment of the assistant State attorney.

"It is up to you, gentlemen," he said, when one of the jurymen asked his opinion. "I do not wish to influence you in any way. I am merely here to help you; but inasmuch as you ask, I might say, for your information, that this case is identical with many others we have handled during this session of the grand jury. The police advise us that there is insufficient evidence to convict.

"If we vote a true bill the taxpayers will be compelled to pay for an expensive trial, at the end of which the defendant will be discharged, and that will be the end of it; while should we vote a no-bill the case may again be brought before the grand jury should the police at any time in the future unearth further evidence.

"Remember, gentlemen, if you vote a true bill now, this case can never again come before the grand jury, and in my humble opinion you will be virtually playing into Farris's hands and insuring him immunity. It is up to you."

The foreman took the vote. A majority favored no bill, and that was the end of that particular case of the People *vs.* Abe Farris. Property interests throughout the city had been protected and real-estate values remained unchanged.

It was the last case on call for that day, and as the jurors hurried out to attend to their neglected businesses Ogden Secor found himself tarrying at his desk in the hope that there might be none present to witness his interview with the girl from Farris's. There was also a growing hope that the girl herself would tire of waiting and depart before he left the jury-room.

The others had gone before he emerged, and it was with a feeling of relief that he realized that this was true, for as he passed through the doorway he saw the trim figure of a young girl sitting in the far corner of the outer room. Her eyes were on the doorway leading to the grand jury room, and as Secor came out she rose and stood waiting him.

He came directly toward her, and as his eyes rested upon her face he ceased to regret that he had asked her to wait. Surely there could be no intentional evil in the owner of such a face. He was confident that it would be an easy matter to guide her into a decent life. As he reached her he found that it was to be rather an embarrassing conversation to open. For a moment he hesitated. It was the girl who first spoke.

"What do you wish of me?" she asked, although she was quite sure that she knew precisely what he wished. While she had waited for him she had quite fully determined her course of action. She was convinced that the "swell job at the Beverly Club" would not be for her, even though the grand jury failed to indict Farris.

A thousand times during the past bitter months she had thrashed out the problem of her life; a thousand times she had determined to seek other employment when she could leave Farris's; and a thousand times she had realized that her life was already ruined past redemption, and that never again could she live among decent people with the constant fear hanging over her that the horrible secret of her past might at any moment be discovered. Better, far better, she thought, to continue in that life until death released her.

But here, she felt, was to be an easier way for a few years at least. Sooner or later this man would tire of her, but in the mean time she would have a good living — it would be much better than either Farris's or the Beverly Club. Possibly she could save enough money to insure the balance of her life against want. She had heard of women like herself who had done this very thing. And so she waited now for the proposal which she was confident Mr. Ogden Secor was about to make.

She knew nothing about this young man — not even his name — nor did she care more about him than to know that he had ample funds with which to defray the cost of an expensive plaything.

"Miss Lynch," said Ogden Secor, "I find the things I wanted to say to you most difficult to say. I scarcely know how to commence. I should hate to offend you."

"No chance," she replied. "You know what I am. There is your answer. Go ahead — get the proposition out of your system."

Though her words were light, she was a trifle nonplused at his method of approach. There was a distinct note of deference in his voice that she had long been unused to from men. Could it be possible that she was mistaken in his intentions? But what else under the sun could he want of her?

"You See," continued Mr. Secor, "I couldn't help but know something of your life from your testimony in there; yet, even though I heard it from your own lips, I find it difficult to believe that it is true — it doesn't seem possible that you could prefer such a life; and I wanted to ask if I might not be of service to you in some way to help you to live differently."

The girl noted the clean, strong face of the young

man before her, the clear eyes, and healthy skin. There was no indication of dissipation or evil habits. She had not spoken to such a man since she came to the city — she had not believed that any clean men lived in the city that she so loathed. She was still inclined, however, to be a trifle skeptical; yet she gave him the benefit of the doubt in her reply.

"I am afraid that it is too late," she said.

"It is never too late," he replied.

"You would not say that if you knew what my early training had been. I was taught to believe that God expected but two things of a woman — to be virtuous, and to become a wife and mother. If she were not virtuous, the second thing became a crime in her — for a woman such as I to marry and bear children were a crime a thousand times more hideous than loss of virtue.

"There was no place on earth for such as I, and no hell of sufficient horror in the hereafter. As far as this life or the next is concerned, I am absolutely and irrevocably lost. I appreciate your kind intentions, but I fear there is nothing to be done."

The girl's words brought Secor up with a sudden and most unpleasant jolt, for he realized that the thing she had said voiced precisely his own views in the matter, or rather what had been his lifelong views up to a few moments before. For the first time in his life he felt that there was something rather unfair, inhuman, and cruel in the sentence that the world passed on its unfortunate sisters.

"I know precisely how you feel," he said at length, making no attempt to lighten the gravity of her sin, "for I, too, have been taught to believe that same thing: but now that I come to deal with a specific case I find that the old theory was of value only in the abstract — it isn't human, and it isn't good sense. There is no reason why you shouldn't lead a decent life if you wish to.

"In fact, that you haven't recently done so is all the more reason that you should commence now. It can't make things any better if you go on as you have been, but as far as you yourself are concerned and those you come in contact with it will be very much better indeed if you live as you should live during the balance of your life."

"Why do you want to help me?" asked the girl suddenly. She had discovered that she had quite unexpectedly lost sight of the motives which she believed had prompted the young man to seek this interview. There had been nothing either in his words or manner to support her suspicions; yet, with her knowledge of men, it was difficult for her to dismiss them.

Secor hesitated a moment before replying, a half smile upon his lips,

"That is a difficult question," he said. "I never did anything of the sort before, and I don't know why I have attempted it now. If I tried to explain the psychology of it I should appear ridiculous, I fear."

"I should like to know," said the girl, "if for no other reason than to learn that I had made a good guess as to what you wanted." She had determined to prove her point for her own satisfaction.

"And what did you think was my reason?" asked Secor.

She looked him straight in the eyes, and without a smile said quite simply:

" To make a date with me."

To say that young Mr. Secor was shocked would have been to put it too mildly by far; but his expression gave no hint of the disappointment and disgust that surged through him.

"And if that were my reason," he asked, "would you

have accepted my — ah — invitation?"

"Why not?" And she was about to add, "Isn't your money as good as anybody's?" But she found herself faltering in her suspicion of this young man, and a sudden sense of shame sent the red blood mantling to her cheek.

For a moment he stood looking straight into her eyes until hers dropped suddenly in confusion.

"I am sorry," he said, "that you should have misconstrued my intentions." His voice held a faint note of sadness and not a little of disappointment. "But as you have, I shall try to give you my real reasons at the risk of appearing silly."

"I wish you would," she said. "I didn't want to think the other, but after my experience with men, it was hard to believe that one of them could go out of his way to perform an unselfish act where a woman was concerned — a woman such as I," she added in a very faint whisper.

"I wanted to help you," said Secor from the moment that I saw your face and heard your voice in the jury-room. I couldn't believe that a girl like you belonged in the underworld. It was not because of the fact that you are a very beautiful girl, but that your face and expression reflect a sweetness of character that seemed entirely out of place in the life you have been leading. There must have been a sudden, subconscious appeal to the protective instinct that is supposed to have been very strong in primitive man — in no other way can I account for the immediate desire I had to save you. Those are my reasons, if you can call them reasons, for asking you to wait here for me. You will doubtless find them as ridiculous as they now seem to me."

The girl's lips trembled as she attempted to speak, and tears came to her eyes so that she had to turn away to hide her emotion. It had been long indeed since a man had spoken to her and of her in this way. Her whole heart went out to this stranger because of those few kindly words — such words as her poor soul had been starving for the want of during the long, hard months of her living death.

"What do you wish me to do?" she asked after she had regained control of her voice.

"Let me help you find employment — that is all that you may accept from any man. It is all that any decent man should offer you," he replied.

"I will do whatever you wish," she said simply.

"I am going away to-morrow," he went on, "to be gone for several weeks. In the mean time I'll give you the name and address of a man who can and will help you to at least temporary employment. Keep in touch with him and when I return we'll see what is best to be done, and what sort of work you are best qualified for."

As he spoke he bad written a name and address upon a leaf of his memorandum-book. He tore the sheet out and handed it to her. Without looking at it she slipped it into her hand-bag.

"And now good-by and good luck," he said, extending his hand to her.

"You must not shake hands with a — with me," she said.

"Don't say that," he replied. "Forget what you have been — you are that no longer. I am wanting to shake hands with an entirely new girl, and to prove that you intend to be a new girl you must let me."

He smiled the clean, wholesome smile that made his strong young face doubly attractive. There was no refusing Ogden Secor anything that he asked when he smiled, and so the girl placed her hand in his.

"This is the ratification of your pledge," he said. "I shall never doubt for a moment that you are keeping it. Until I return, then," and bowing he left her there, a new hope and a great happiness in her heart.

If one good man could forgive her her past, there must be others. Possibly the world would not be so hard upon her after all. Maybe there was a chance for her to live as she wanted to live, and to find the happiness that she had so craved, and which she had thought was lost forever.

Suddenly she recalled that she did not know the name of the man who had just left her. Well, that could easily be ascertained. She had the name and address of his friend. She would go to him at once and take any employment that he could find for her. She would work for a bare living, if necessary, rather than go back to the old life. She would do anything for the man who had spoken to her as this young stranger had spoken.

Eagerly she opened her hand-bag and withdrew the little slip of paper. As she read the name a cold wave of disappointment and bitterness chilled and blighted the new happiness and hope that had filled her being.

The name on the paper was "Rev. Theodore Pursen."

Chapter V

A FRIEND IN NEED

*I*T was a very disheartened girl who found her way out of the criminal court building and across the Dearborn Street Bridge to the Loop. She was wondering if her new friend were of the same type of reformer as the Rev. Mr. Pursen. Would he want her to narrate the story of her rescue for the Sunday editions upon his return?

Then it occurred to her that she would not see him when he came back to the city, for she had no idea who he might be, and she certainly would not go to the Rev. Mr. Pursen to find out. It began to look as though she had made a false start after all on her road to a new life.

At Lake and Dearborn she stopped to purchase an evening paper, and in the entrance to a near-by building she sought among the want ads for a likely boarding-house. She found an address far out on the South Side, and a moment later boarded a Cottage Grove Avenue car at Wabash Avenue.

As she rode South she tried to reach some definite decision as to her future. She could go back to the old life, and the young man would never know. The chances are that he would not care if he did know.

His act had been prompted by but the passing kindness of a moment. If he ever thought of her again, it would be but to inquire of his friend the Rev. Mr. Pursen if she had applied to him for aid, and finding that she had not, he would promptly forget all about the incident.

As she speculated upon her future, her eyes wandered aimlessly over the printed page of close-set want ads in the paper in her hand.

Presently a notice caught her attention:

WANTED — Neat girl for general office work; small wages to start; experience unnecessary. Apply Kesner Building.

"Why not try it?" she thought. "He'll never know, of course, but he was on the square. He wanted to help me, and I can't believe that he is like Pursen. He wanted to give me a chance to be the kind of girl he thought I looked like, and why shouldn't I be? I can do that much, surely, when all my inclinations lie in that direction. I haven't wanted to be bad, God knows; and I guess I've been a fool to think that I had to keep on that way just because I had started."

At Twenty-Fourth Street a pimply-faced young man boarded the car. As he walked forward toward the front platform, a lighted cigarette in his nicotine-stained fingers, be turned to stare into the face of every woman in the car. When he came opposite the girl from Farris's he stopped with a broad grin upon his unclean face.

"Why, hello there, Mag!" he cried. "When did you get out?" And with the words he plumped into the seat at her side.

"This afternoon, Eddie," she replied quietly.

"Where to now?" he asked.

"I'm on my way uptown to find a boarding-place."

"Got a new job already?" he asked, surprised.

"I'm cuttin' that out, Eddie," she said. "I'm goin' to be on the square after this."

"Forget it," he grinned.

"On the dead."

"Who's keepin' you?" he persisted.

"Myself."

"May Beverley asked me to look you up," he remarked. "She says you promised to come there."

"I didn't think she'd want me after that Farris business," replied the girl.

The young man laughed.

"Huh! What does she care? She ain't got no love for Farris, and besides a chicken with an angel face like yours can get in anywhere in the burg. But on the dead, Mag, you're a boob not to get your hooks onto some rich gazimbat. I know a gink right now that'll pass me out five hundred bones any time for a squab like you. Say the word and I'll split with you."

The girl looked at the man for a moment, and then turned and gazed out of the window.

"That's right; think it over," said Eddie. "It's a good proposition and that ain't no dream. He's not exactly pretty, but he's there with a bundle of kale that would choke the Panama. He'd set you up in a swell apartment, plaster sparklers all over you, and give you a year-after-next model eight-lunger and a shuffer. You'd be the only cheese on Mich. Boul."

The girl knew that Eddie was not romancing; and here she had been thinking that she could not even get into the Beverley Club. Here was easy money — riches even — just for the taking; and she would be no worse for it than she already was.

She looked again at the man beside her, and as she looked she found herself comparing him with the young man she had last talked with. He, too, had come to her with an offer. She glanced at the want ad lying face-up in the paper on her lap.

"Five dollars a week," she mused. "Six at the most."

"What's that?" asked Eddie. "I didn't getcha."

Eddie was smiling at her. She saw his smile, but beyond it she saw the smile of that other young man. Eddie would have felt pained could he have read the unvoiced comparison that shot into the girl's mind as she looked at Eddie's yellow-toothed, unwholesome smirk.

"Well?" asked Eddie at last. "Shall I frame up a date?"

"No," said the girl, "I think I've got a swell job already. Good-by, Eddie; here's where I get off."

She found the boarding-house, and after paying a week's board in advance returned to the Loop, seeking the Kesner Building. On the eighteenth floor she found the room number given in the want ad.

"There have been fifteen other applicants already," said the man to whom she had been directed by a typist near the door of the office; "but I haven't decided on any one in particular yet — there'll be as many more in to-morrow morning. Have you had any experience?"

"No; the advertisement said that was unnecessary," she replied.

"Yes, of course; but with so many applicants I would naturally prefer to choose an experienced girl. What have you been doing?"

The girl hesitated.

"Nothing," she said finally; "I have just come from the country."

"What is your name?"

"Lathrop — June Lathrop," she answered, giving him her true name; for with her decision to commence life anew she had also decided to do so under her true colors. There would be nothing in her future, she had determined, that could bring odium upon her father's name.

"Well Miss Lathrop," said he, "to be frank, you're the most likely looking of the applicants so far. Most of them have had experience, but that doesn't count much against natural intelligence, and unless I'm way off you've got that. I'll tell you what, you come back here tomorrow morning about nine-thirty, and if no one I like better has shown up by that time the job's yours. Good afternoon."

For three months June Lathrop folded and enclosed circulars on the eighteenth floor of the Kesner Building at the princely salary of six dollars a week. As her board and room at the place she had first selected cost her seven dollars a week, it required but a rudimentary knowledge of higher mathematics to convince her that she would either have to change positions or boarding-houses. She chose the latter alternative.

The change brought her into a neighborhood perilously close to the red-light district. Several times she saw women she had known in that other life. They passed her upon the street, clothed in clinging silk and starred with many a scintillating gem. June was careful to see that they did not have a chance to recognize her.

Her clothes were becoming a trifle shabby; but they were neat, and were worn with that indefinable air that some women can impart to rags.

Not once yet had she regretted the step she had taken. For the first time in months she felt a growing interest in life and a quiet contentment that was almost happiness — as near to happiness at least as she ever expected to attain.

She often smiled sadly to herself in recalling upon how slight a thing the turning in her life had hinged

— the clean smile and kindly interest of a stranger, a man whose name, even, she did not know.

Early in her career upon the eighteenth floor of the Kesner Building June had discovered that the road to higher wages paralleled the acquirement of special training. Any one could fold and enclose circulars. There were always thousands of young girls to be employed at a moments notice for this class of work; but even here, she discovered, expertness demanded and received the highest wages. So she made it a point to become expert.

At the end of the second month she could handle a greater volume of work in a day than any other girl in the department, and with a lower percentage of errors. Her wages were advanced to seven dollars, and she was entrusted with the more important work of the department.

In the same room with her were several typists and on the floor below many stenographers. June discovered that the poorest paid typist earned a dollar a week more than she — or at least received that much more.

She determined to become a typist, and with that end in view practiced during the noon hour each day under the guidance of one of the regular typists. From her she learned that some of the stenographers downstairs received as much as seventy-five dollars a month — almost three times her wage!

That evening June enrolled in a night-school where she could study stenography. The venture necessitated a curtailment of expenses — it meant walking to and from her work and finding a still cheaper room than that she had. Her new lodgings were nearer the Loop. Here she had a tiny gas-stove, where she cooked her slender meals — two a day, some days.

At night she practiced and studied. In a month she could take ordinary dictation and transcribe ninety per cent of it quite as it had been dictated. Without being aware of it she had become some forty per cent more efficient than most stenographers ever become; yet she felt that she was far from the proficiency required to obtain or hold a position.

Then the blow fell. Her careful attention to her work, in the circularizing department — her expertness — lost her position for her. It happens every day in the departments of big businesses in every city. A slack season came. Expenses must be curtailed. The head of the house conferred with the manager of her department. The pay-roll was the first item to be considered in reducing expenses — it always is. Likewise it was the last thing.

"How many girls can you spare at this season of the year, Mr. Brown?" asked the head of the house.

"We can cut the force in two," replied Mr. Brown, not because he thought so, but because he thought the head of the house would like to have him say it. Mr. Brown had been up against this same thing twice a year since he had assumed the management of the department. He had found it far easier to coincide with the wishes of his superior, especially when the hysteria of retrenchment was abroad; later he could employ other girls to bring his department up to a respectable working basis — after the head of the house had transferred his attention and hysteria to another department or another field of endeavor.

The head of the house glanced down the pay-roll, a copy of which Mr. Brown had handed him.

"H-m!" he said. "Seven dollars! Seven dollars is too much for this class of work, Mr. Brown. When I started this business I had but one employee — a girl. She and I did all the work. I used to work eighteen and twenty hours a day, and if I had made seven dollars a week clear the first year I should have been delighted. She worked nearly every night and Saturday afternoons as well, and did it for three dollars a week. You are paying your help altogether too much. I see you have three girls in this department who are receiving seven dollars a week — we will start with them."

And he made three little x's — one before the name of each of the three. So June lost her job. When Mr. Brown told her that he would not need her after the following Saturday she was dumfounded.

"Hasn't my work been satisfactory?" she asked.

"Yes," replied Mr. Brown; and then as well as he could he explained the necessity for cutting down the force: but just why it was necessary to lay off his most efficient help he did not attempt to explain.

That night and for many days thereafter June scanned the want columns of the papers. She wrote in reply to blind ads — letters that never received a response. She called in answer to those that gave an address, but there was always something they wanted that she lacked.

Quite often the positions were filled before she applied, and then she discovered that she must wait upon the corner near the office of the afternoon newspaper from which she obtained her leads, seize one of the first copies that came onto the street, and hasten to the addresses of the more likely appearing ads if she would be in time to obtain a first hearing.

In this way she managed, during the ensuing three or four months to pick up half a dozen temporary positions at wages ranging from five to nine dollars a week, but fully half the time she was idle. She had been compelled to give up night-school, but she still practiced stenography at home; and her afternoons, when she was out of employment, she spent at the employment bureaus of various typewriter companies gaining speed on machines of different makes.

She had not sufficient confidence as yet to apply for a position as typist — she was too inexperienced to know that this is the sole asset of the majority of typists.

Four months after she lost her position in the Kesner Building she was working in the bindery department of a small job printing establishment at four dollars a week. Her clothes were by this time far too shabby for her to hope to obtain an office position; nor was there any immediate likelihood that she would be able to save sufficient money from her wages ever to purchase other clothing. But even now she retained her courage, though hope was rapidly succumbing.

Poor and insufficient food had left its mark upon her pallid, emaciated cheeks and dark-ringed eyes. She had made no friends among her coworkers. The good girls she avoided from a sense of shame in her past; the others, with their cheap immoralities, disgusted her. She would be one thing or the other — all good or all bad — and so she could not abide those who sailed under false colors, assuming a respectability that they did not have.

She still retained sufficient beauty to make her noticeable among other girls. It was her sole possession of value. One day she had an opportunity to cash it. The man who ran the print-shop often walked through the bindery inspecting the work. On several occasions he stopped and spoke to June about the job that she happened to be engaged upon. He was a middle-aged man, rather good-looking. There was little or no indication of dissipation upon his face, and yet June knew that he was a hunter — she had heard snatches of conversation among the other girls; conversation that made her blush, hardened as she thought she was.

One afternoon the forewoman told her that "the boss" wanted to see her in his office. She hastened to respond to the summons.

Her employer smiled pleasantly as she entered.

"Sit down," he said, indicating a chair beside his desk.

June did as he bid.

"How long have you been with us?" he asked.

"Two weeks," she replied.

"I have been noticing your work — and you," said the man. "I think that you are not getting enough wages. I believe that we can fix it up so that you can earn ten dollars a week — how would that strike you?"

The girl's eyes narrowed, but the man did not notice.

"I should be glad if I could earn ten dollars a week," she replied.

"Well, suppose you take dinner with me to-night and we'll talk it over — I'm too busy just now. Well, what do you say?"

June looked him straight in the eyes, and then she laughed. She thought of the apartment on Michigan Avenue, the eight-cylinder touring-car, the chauffeur, the diamonds — of all that she had refused seven months ago.

"You poor boob," she said. "You poor, cheap boob, you!"

The man turned scarlet. He tried to say something, but the words stuck in his throat.

June rose from her chair.

"Give me my time, please. I've heard that there were men like you. Before I went to work I thought they were all like you; but in all the offices I have worked — and I've worked in a lot of them — you're the first man that ever made a raw crack like that to me. If you had had the nerve to come right out and say what you wanted of me I might at least have had a little respect for you; but to try to work that rotten old cradle-robbing dinner-game on me! And offering me ten dollars a week and work all day in the bindery to boot! Give me my four dollars and let me get out of here!"

For two weeks June sought another position in vain. Her money was gone, and she owed for a week's room rent. She had no food or prospects of food. She had not eaten for twenty-four hours; and then, as fate would have it, she met Eddie on the street — Eddie of the pimply face, the unclean nails, and the stained fingers.

"For the love o' Mike!" exclaimed Eddie. "You?"

"Surest thing you know, Eddie," replied the girl, laughing.

"The swellest-lookin' chicken on the line — in rags!" he said. "What's the idea, Mag? Got a job as one of them new she-cops and doin' a little gum-shoe work in disguise?"

"No, Eddie; I'm out of a job."

Sudden enlightenment dawned upon Eddie's countenance.

"Bein' on the square hasn't got you much, eh?"

"No, Eddie; it hasn't got me anything except an awful appetite and nothing to satisfy it with."

The young man looked into her face searchingly.

"You hungry, Mag!"

She didn't deny it.

He grasped her by the arm.

"You come along with me," he commanded. "I know a joint round the corner where we can feed up swell on four bits, and that's all I got just now."

The girl drew back.

"No, Eddie," she said; "I can't sponge."

"Forget it," he cried. "Do you suppose I'll see an old pal hungry when I got the price? Not me!"

And then, as she still demurred, his expression changed.

"Oh." he said, "I forgot. You're on the square now, so you'd be ashamed to be seen with a dip like me —

that's it. Well, I don't know but you're right. You can't be too careful."

"That's not it, Eddie, and you know it," she cried. "But I've been trying so hard to make good! I haven't asked anybody for help, and I've been on the square all the time. I hate to have to fall back on charity now."

"Charity nothin'!" he exploded. "You'd do as much for me if I was down and out. Come along now, and when you get the price you can feed me up in return if you feel that way about it."

And so they went together to the joint around the corner where they could get a swell feed for two for fifty cents.

"What do you think of this virtue lay by this time?" asked Eddie after they had partially satisfied the cravings of the inner man and woman.

"I guess it's its own reward all right enough," replied the girl.

Eddie was silent for a moment.

"Do you remember me tellin' you about an old bloke the last time I seen you?" he asked presently.

"Yes."

"That proposition's still open."

She reached across the table and laid her hand upon his stained fingers.

"Don't, Eddie," she said. "I'm trying hard to fight the temptation to go back where there is plenty of easy money, and good clothes, and enough to eat. I want to be on the square, though, Eddie, so don't make it harder for me."

He patted her hand.

"You're the real goods, Mag," he said. I thought you was just four-flushin' that time you told me you'd quit the gay life, but I guess it takes more'n a four-flush for a girl like you to wear them clothes and starve to boot just for the sake of bein' decent. I won't say nothin' more about that proposition; but if I can help you any other old way, why, you got my number.

"Gee!" he continued, "I wish I had your nerve. I tried a dozen times to quit and be decent. But the easy money down here always got me — that and the coke. Tell me all you been doin' since I seen you, and what's went wrong that you couldn't get a job."

She related her experiences; closing with an account of the print-shop man.

"The cheap skate!" exclaimed Eddie. "Gimme his number, and I'll hike down his way to-morrow and touch him for all he's got in his jeans — it'll teach him a lesson."

"No, Eddie, that wouldn't be setting me a very good example of being decent, would it?"

The man laughed.

"But say," he said, "why is it you don't go after a swell steno job? You say they told you down at the typewriter joint that you was the real cheese and ought to hold any job you could cop off."

"Yes, I know they did," she replied, "but they intimated that they couldn't send me out in answer to a call unless I had better clothes, and you can't buy much on four dollars a week, Eddie, especially if you only get the four some weeks."

Eddie sat for a moment deep in thought. Then he rose and reached for his hat.

"You sit tight here for about ten minutes, Mag," he said, "and I'll be right back. I got some business up the street. I want to see you again when I come back. You won't duck, will you?"

"I'll wait for you, Eddie," she replied.

The man stopped at the cashier's desk and paid the two checks, then he hurried out into the brilliantly lighted street.

It was fifteen minutes before he returned, and when

he took his place at the table opposite her the girl did not know that he no longer wore a diamond stickpin, a watch of gold, and a diamond ring.

"Here," he said, shoving a roll of bills across the table to her. "Here's a stake for them swell clothes you need to land a decent job."

Chapter VI

SECOR'S FIANCEE

Long before Mr. Ogden Secor returned to the city after his grand jury service had terminated and released him to attend to his own affairs, he had completely forgotten the girl from Farris's and his promise of assistance to her.

It was fully a month after his return that he was reminded of the affair by the sight of the Rev. Mr. Pursen at the home of Secor's fiancée where both had dropped in of a late afternoon.

"By the way, Mr. Pursen," said Secor, "did a girl I sent to you for assistance ever apply? She was the girl from Farris's in that case that was brought before the grand jury of which I was foreman."

"No," said the Rev. Mr. Pursen, "she did not come to me. I went to her the very day that Farris was arrested and offered to help her; but I found her entirely unresponsive to my advances. In fact, she seemed totally depraved, and though I labored with her I was finally forced to the conclusion that she was one of those hopelessly lost women which nothing but death can remove from the evil life they cling to by preference."

"Strange," said Mr. Secor; "she completely deceived me. I could have sworn that she was not innately vicious, and that if given a chance she might easily have been helped to a better way of living."

"No," said the Rev. Mr. Pursen; "I did my poor, weak best; but it was all to no avail."

"Too bad," said Mr. Secor, and that would have been the end of it had not fate been planning the perpetration of an odd trick upon him.

Sophia Welles entered at that moment, and both men arose to greet her.

"I have come to beg again, Miss Welles," said Mr. Pursen. "I find that our Society for the Uplift of Erring Women is sadly in need of funds. The secretary's salary is a month in arrears; the stenographer and the two investigators have not been paid for two weeks, and the rent is several days overdue."

"Well, well," murmured Miss Welles sympathetically, "that is too bad. We must certainly do something at once. How much do you need, and what can you rely upon from other sources?"

"We need about two hundred dollars at once," replied the clergyman, "and some arrangement would be very advantageous that would assure us of a permanent income of two hundred and fifty or three hundred dollars per month."

"I will subscribe fifty dollars toward the emergency fund at once," said Miss Welles. She looked expectantly toward Mr. Secor.

"What is the nature of the work done by the society?" asked that gentleman.

"The name of the society is self-explanatory," returned Mr. Pursen. "The Society for the Uplift of Erring Women."

"Roughly," Mr. Secor inquired, "how does it function?"

"Our investigators call upon the women whose cases come to our attention — usually through Municipal Court records — and endeavor to prevail upon them to attend our Monday evening Uplift Circle. The meetings are held in the church every Monday except during July and August. Here we enjoy a short song service, followed by prayer, and then the women listen to helpful talks by the noble women who are sacrificing their Monday evenings to their poor, fallen sisters."

"Do many of the women you seek to aid attend these meetings?" asked Mr. Secor.

"Unfortunately, no," admitted Mr. Pursen; "possibly five or six, on an average, I should say. The unfortunate part of it is that they seem to have so little real desire to embrace the opportunity we are offering them to begin life anew that seldom if ever do the same women attend our Uplift Circle a second time. You have no conception, Mr. Secor, how discouraging is labor of this nature — the utter indifference and ingratitude of those we would help is the first and greatest obstacle to our work."

"Just how would you help them, practically?" inquired Mr. Secor.

"By contact with good women; by the beauties of Scripture; by helpful suggestions and example; by impressing upon them their degradation; by — ah —"

" Do you find remunerative employment for them?" asked Mr. Secor.

"We have not gone thus far as yet, though that is the ultimate object, of course."

"I should think that it would be the primary object. Between meetings they go back and earn their livings in the old way — if you have accomplished anything it is undone at once."

"It is difficult to find people who will employ these women once we explain the sort of people they are," replied Mr. Pursen; "but that we hope to be able to do when we have sufficient funds to employ more assistants."

"You have placed none of them in decent employment, then?" asked Mr. Secor.

"Not as yet — it takes time to accomplish great reforrns — Rome was not —"

"Yes, of course," interrupted Mr. Secor; "but, looking at the matter from a purely business standpoint, I cannot see how you are going to raise sufficient funds to carry on any work until you have accomplished something practical with what you have. If four or five paid workers, with the assistance of a number of volunteers, have been unable to effect the regeneration of not a single woman in the six or eight months that the society has been organized, I should consider it a rather risky investment to subscribe any considerable amount for the continuation of the work.

"I don't wish to discourage you," continued Mr. Secor kindly, "but charities to be effective must be treated just as one would treat a business proposition. If a given charity is not producing results it would be better to divert our money to other channels — there are several well-managed charities, I understand, that are doing considerable practical good."

"Then you think that the Society for the Uplift of Erring Women is poorly managed?" asked Mr. Pursen a trifle acridly.

"It may be and it may not — there are some things which cannot be done — impractical things. This may be one of them; or the methods of the society may be faulty. Of course I am in no position to judge, nor do I wish to criticize."

"I can assure you that my cousin, Miss Peebles, is a

very conscientious woman," said Mr. Pursen, "and is doing a noble work intelligently."

"Oh," said Mr. Secor; "I ask your pardon. I did not know that the secretary of the society is your cousin."

"She is," continued Mr. Pursen, "and the other active workers in the society are relatives of the good women who are aiding us in our thankless task."

"You mean by active workers —"

"Those who are on salary — not being financially able to devote their time to the work gratuitously," explained Mr. Pursen.

"I think," said Miss Welles, "that the society is doing a very noble work under most adverse conditions, and that we should do all in our power to help it financially, as well as to give it our moral support. It is very easy, Ogden, to criticize."

"I am sorry," said Mr. Secor, "if I have seemed to disparage the work of the society; but knowing as I do that it is rather a pet of yours, Sophia, I wanted to do something really worth while for it — if my money would do any good. There is no value in throwing money away for sentiment when there are so many places where it can be used to practical advantage.

"I should like very much to talk with Miss Peebles, and if I find that there is good foundation for the belief that fallen women can be really saved or benefited through your organization, I shall be most happy to subscribe toward an endowment fund, and influence my friends to do likewise."

"That is very kind of you, Mr. Secor," said Mr. Pursen, relaxing as he scented a substantial donation.

"Where is the office of the society?" asked Mr. Secor. "I shall make it a point to see Miss Peebles to-morrow."

"The office is in the church," said Mr. Pursen. "You will find Miss Peebles there about eleven o'clock. She is usually there between eleven and twelve daily."

"I thought from your reference to rent," remarked Mr. Secor, "that the society probably had a down-town office."

"No," replied Mr. Pursen; "we felt that as long as the society would have to pay rent it would be better to give this rent to the church rather than to outsiders, and we have made the amount very much smaller than the society could have obtained similar space for in the Loop."

"Oh," said Mr. Secor, "I see. Well, then, if possible, I shall call upon Miss Peebles to-morrow; but do not tell her to expect me, for I may find business engagements will prevent my seeing her before the first of the week."

"I hope not," Mr. Pursen said; "for I am sure that Miss Peebles can explain the work and scope of the society much more interestingly than I, in my poor, weak way."

"We might look up that girl from Farris's again," suggested Mr. Secor, "and see what Miss Peebles can do for her."

"She is too degraded, I am afraid, ever to respond to the kind offices of good men and women. I think that she prefers her present life, sad as it may seem to us. Poor thing! I tried so hard to win her to godliness.

"But I must he going, now. I am so very glad to have met you again, Mr. Secor. May we not hope to see you oftener at our little church gatherings? In my poor, weak way I shall endeavor to make you welcome."

"Just a moment, Mr. Pursen," said Miss Welles, "until I make out a check for the Uplift Society."

After the Rev. Mr. Pursen had departed with his check Sophia turned to Secor.

"Isn't he splendid?" she exclaimed.

So noble and sincere in his desire to better his fellow man! So magnanimous in his practical relations with the poor creatures of the under-world!"

"Rather nice chap to have for a cousin, I should say, were one in quest of remunerative employment with short hours," replied Mr. Secor with a trace of dryness."

Miss Welles looked at her fiancée sharply.

"How perfectly unkind, Ogden," she exclaimed. "Really, I'd never have thought it of you. Mr. Pursen is one of nature's own noblemen."

"All right, Sophie; we won't quarrel about Mr. Pursen, although I must say that if his attitude toward that girl I spoke to him about is a decent sample of his magnanimous practicality, or whatever you called it, I am afraid it won't carry him very far in that class of work."

"And you won't help him?" she asked.

"If you wish me to, yes," he replied; "but if you were not interested I should feel that I'd rather contribute my money directly to the support of his indigent cousin and his church rather than through the medium of the Society for the Uplift of Erring Women. He'd get it all then, and wouldn't have to whack up with the indigent relatives of the noble women who sacrifice their Monday evenings, except during July and August, to the uplift of their less-fortunate sisters."

"You are entirely horrid to-day, Ogden," pouted Miss Welles. "You do not like Mr. Pursen."

"Bless you, child, I don't know him. I've met him here perhaps a half dozen times — here, and in the newspapers. About all I've noticed about him is the poor, weak way he has of getting into print."

Miss Welles flushed. She had heard that criticism of her hero before.

"You are just like father," she said.

"He can't, or won't understand how much Mr. Pursen shrinks from the unpleasant notoriety his great reform work forces upon him. Like you, father seems to imagine that he courts publicity, while as a matter of fact he suffers it solely because he cannot avoid it, and because he knows that only by bringing the conditions of vice that exist in the city clearly before the people can they be awakened to the gravity of the issue which confronts them. I think the fact that he goes on and on regardless of the frequency with which the newspapers drag his name into publicity is one of the finest things about him — it proves conclusively his sincerity and his manly courage."

"All right, Sophie," replied Secor with one of his pleasant smiles, "if he succeeds in saving a single woman during his lifetime he will not have lived in vain, and there is every reason to hope for the best — Mr. Pursen is still a very young man."

The talk drifted then from Mr. Pursen and reform to more personal and intimate matters. They discussed their plans for the future. Secor broached the subject of a wedding date for the hundredth time, and for the hundredth time Sophia Welles could not bring herself to be very definite in the matter.

She fully intended to marry Ogden Secor. She had not worked laboriously a whole year to that end with any intention of relinquishing her prize now that she had won it; but Miss Welles was in no great haste to wed. She loved Secor as well as she knew how. He was quite good-looking, had plenty of wealth, and a social position second to none in the city. Had he had nothing but the social position, Miss Welles could not have found it in her heart to give him up, but with such a combination of assets he was by far the best catch in many a season.

She had come from a small Indiana town where her father had made several fortunes in the automobile industry — saving them all and investing them wisely. She did not need to marry for money, though an alliance that would combine the wealth that would one day be hers with that of a wealthy husband was not to be ignored. What she did need was a stepping-stone to the social position she craved, but could not attain on the strength of her own name. Both she and her mother considered Ogden Secor an ideal stepping-stone, though neither had ever mentioned such a thing to the other.

As a matter of fact the Welleses were extremely nice people. Refined, educated cultured. Much nicer, if the truth could have found a champion of sufficient bravery to admit it, than many of the families to whose homes the feminine contingent of the Welles household craved entree; but their name was unknown in this new environment.

It had never graced a special brand of ham; it had never been intimately related and for generations with the filth and crime of the politics of the municipality; it did not blazon itself before the public eye from above the doorways of a hundred ten-cent lunch-counters — no, the Welleses were new, unknown; they did not belong.

But they meant to.

Ogden Secor had always known nice girls, pretty girls, rich girls. He did not succumb to the wiles of Sophia Welles at first sight, for she had nothing new to offer him; but she had that way with her which some women have of suggesting to a man a manner of proprietorship over them — a something that appeals to the protective instinct of the male.

It is done insidiously; you cannot put your finger on a single act that typifies it; yet before long the man comes to feel, without thinking about it, perhaps, that the woman belongs to him in a way. Then she plays her trump card. Just when she has him resting easily and comfortably in the belief that she looks to him for advice and guidance, she traps him into an attempt to exercise the power he thinks is his. Then she bowls him over merrily and does precisely as she pleases.

What is the result? Take away from a man by force something that he has come to believe he possessed, and you create a burning desire for the thing — though maybe before he would not have given a nickel for it.

So, when Ogden Secor discovered that Miss Welles admitted not his proprietorship over her, he immediately craved a real proprietorship, and the result was he discovered that he loved her.

They had been engaged now for three months, but the wedding day seemed as far in the future as ever. Miss Welles was having an excellent time as the fiancée of Mr. Ogden Secor. Already she had tasted of the fruits of conquest. Doors had opened to her that had previously been impregnable. She was in no haste to relinquish her freedom.

The sudden death of the elder Secor early in the spring had, of course, necessitated a delay in the wedding plans; for both Miss and Mrs. Welles desired a pretentious ceremony. It seemed now that a year at least must elapse before the marriage could take place.

As for Mr. Secor, he attempted to persuade his betrothed to slip away with him and be quietly married in some nearby town. Her father and mother could accompany them, and everything would be regular and lovely. He hated the idea of "the circus," as he called the affair the two women were planning.

But they would not listen to him.

Several times during the winter Secor met the Rev. Mr. Pursen at Miss Welles's. The more he saw of him the less he liked him, and the more he let Miss Welles see that he disliked her "parson," the more loyal she became to him.

"One would think that you were engaged to Pursen

instead of to me," complained Mr. Secor on one occasion. "He is becoming a regular pest. I can scarcely ever find an opportunity to see you alone. Doesn't he know that we are engaged? Hasn't he any sense?"

"He has a great deal of sense, Ogden, she replied," and he knows that we are engaged. He also knows that you do not like him. He has told me so."

"Then why does he persist in hanging around while I am here, Sophie?" he demanded.

"I think he wants to show his friendliness toward you and to win your friendship. I think it is perfectly sweet and noble of him — a sort of martyrship to brotherly love, as it were."

Carefully edited, Mr. Secor's reply would read: "Oh, piffle!"

"Ogden! How can you!" she cried, "I didn't know that you had such an uncharitable strain in your make-up."

"Clay feet will out," he laughed good-naturedly; "but really, Sophie, I'm sorry I was nasty. Forgive me, and I'll do my best to like your parson — in my poor, weak way."

"You'll have to like him, Ogden," she replied, "for we are bound to see a great deal of him! In the work that I am trying to do his assistance is invaluable — I am sure that the three of us can accomplish a great deal of good in this city could we but work in harmony — whole-heartedly for the uplift."

"Anything to make you happy Sophie," he said, and then the conversation turned to other things.

When he left she watched him as he walked to the curb and entered his car. Miss Welles was very proud of her fiancée. She noted his splendid carriage, his strong face and well-set head; and then she sighed. She wished that he understood her hopes and aspirations, and was in sympathy with them as was — well — Mr.

Pursen, for example.

He understood.

She found herself, quite unexpectedly, wondering why fate had not given Mr. Pursen a fat bank account and an old and socially honored name. How much more he could have accomplished, thus bucklered for the fight!

Chapter VII

JUNE'S EMPLOYER

*L*ate in December Mr. Secor was called to New York on a matter of business.

"I'll be gone two or three weeks, Stickler," he said to his office manager; "and it'll be an excellent time to break in Miss Smith's successor. She'll be with us until the first of January, and that'll give her time to coach whoever you employ in her stead. Be sure you get a young woman of intelligence, and have her well versed in her duties before I return — I won't want to have to suffer the sorrows incident to breaking in a new stenographer myself with a bunch of accumulated matter piled up and waiting for me."

"Yes, sir," replied Mr. Stickler; "I'll see that you have a second Miss Smith if there's one to be found in the city. Too bad she had to go and get married — just when she was becoming invaluable."

"Very inconsiderate of her, Stickler, I'm sure," said Secor, laughing.

So Mr. Stickler inserted want ads in three papers and

telephoned to the employment departments of three typewriter manufacturers. And it so happened that the following day June Lathrop, decently clothed with the money from Eddie's jewelry, walked into one of these departments, asking for an assignment.

The woman in charge looked up with a smile.

"Why, good morning, Miss Lathrop," she said. "Where in the world have you been? I thought we'd lost you entirely."

She had never before realized what a really beautiful girl Miss Lathrop was. A few months since she had explained to her in as kindly a way as possible that it would be impossible for her to place her in the class of offices to which they catered unless she could come better clothed. She had not seen her again after that interview until now, and she had often wondered if she had offended the girl.

"Oh, I've been doing temporary work about town," answered June; "but now I want a chance at a permanent position. Haven't you something that you could send me out on? Something really good."

"I've just the thing, Miss Lathrop," replied the woman, fingering through a number of index cards in a little box on her desk.

Presently she found what she sought, and for a moment was busy transcribing the contents of the card to a blank form.

"Here," she said finally; "go to this number in the Railway Exchange and ask for Mr. Stickler. He wants a girl of more experience than you have had, but I really believe that you are fully competent to fill the position satisfactorily, and I have told him so in this note. I have asked him to give you a trial."

"I don't know how I can thank you enough," cried the girl. "I shall make good, for I *must* make good."

"Good luck, then," called the woman, as June left.

In the Railway Exchange Building June found the suite number she sought. The door to the main office was open, and she did not see the lettering upon it as she entered. She wondered what the nature of the business might be, but that it was profitable was evidenced by the thick carpet upon the floor of the outer office; and by the simple elegance of the desks at which a number of clerks were working.

At the information desk June asked for Mr. Stickler, presenting her note of introduction to the office-boy in charge. He was a tall, somber youth of sixteen who looked fully twenty-one. He eyed June from beneath stern brows, and then slunk silently toward a mahogany door upon the opposite side of the general office. Here he turned cautiously to cast a sudden, veiled look of suspicion in the girl's direction.

"How perfectly weird," she thought. "He makes me feel as though I were a sneak-thief."

Three minutes later June turned with a little jump to find the young man standing just behind her scowling down upon her in the most malevolent manner. He had left the private office by another door and entered the reception hall from the main corridor of the building.

"Oh!" she exclaimed; "you startled me."

The youth almost smiled.

"Come!" he whispered. "Follow me," and on silent feet he led her toward the private office across the room.

Here she was ushered into the presence of Mr. Stickler — a bald-headed man with a thick neck and close-set eyes. At sight of the girl's face Mr. Stickler beamed pleasantly.

"Good morning," he said. "Have a chair. You come well recommended, I see. Mrs. Carson has never failed to furnish us with the most competent help that we have had. She tells me that you have had little practical experience; but she is positive that you can do our work most satisfactorily."

"If it is not too technical I am sure I can," replied June.

"There is nothing about it but what you can learn quickly if you set yourself to it," replied Mr. Stickler kindly. He had interviewed a dozen applicants already and he was tiring of the job. This was the first who had been good to look at; and good looks were a primary requisite to employment under Mr. Stickler. June's face had won more than half the battle for her.

"Would you mind taking a little dictation now and transcribing it for me, as a sort of test, you know?" he asked.

"Not at all; I should be very glad to," she replied.

"Good!" he exclaimed. "There are many applicants who will not take a test. They say it is unfair."

"It is as fair for one as another," she replied. "I cannot see how you are to judge as to my qualifications in any other way."

Mr. Stickler drew a note-book and pencil from his desk, and June removed her wraps and gloves. For five minutes he dictated continuously and rather rapidly; but he enunciated his words distinctly, and not once did June find it necessary to stop him or ask for a repetition.

When he had finished he sat back in his chair and smiled at her. He had purposely made the test unusually hard, for he had decided that the girl would do — she was too good-looking to be lost — and so he wanted an excuse in case she fell down on the test. If he made it exceptionally difficult, it would not prove that she was incompetent should she make numerous errors, for even an easy test is a nerve-racking experience, and the best of stenographers often fall down through nervousness.

Of course, if the result proved that she was absolutely hopeless, he could not employ her; but if she showed the slightest indication of ability, he would give her a trial.

"Do you think you got it?" he asked.

"Why, of course!" she replied, surprised.

"Good! I made it as hard as I could. If you can transcribe that with less than ten per cent errors, you will be doing splendidly for one entirely unaccustomed to my dictation and the terms I used."

"Where can I find a machine?" she asked.

Mr. Stickler touched a bell.

"Miss Smith," he said to the young lady who entered in response to his summons, "this is Miss Lathrop. She has just taken a test. Will you let her use your machine, please, to transcribe for a few minutes?"

"Certainly. Come with me, Miss Lathrop." And she led June to a small room off the private office.

In ten minutes June knocked upon Mr. Stickler's door.

"Come in," he called, and as he saw who it was: "Stuck?" he asked with a smile.

"No, indeed; I've finished."

"Well, well; that's fine. Let me see it."

June handed him a typewritten sheet, standing before him as he scanned it.

"Excellent!" he said when he had finished reading it. "Excellent! Not an error. I think I need look no further, Miss Lathrop, if we can arrange the question of wages satisfactorily. Be seated, please. Now, what do you believe would satisfy you to start?"

"Oh, I'd rather leave that to you," said June.

"Miss Smith has been with us for five years," said Mr. Stickler. "She is leaving on the first to be married. We pay her twenty-five dollars a week. On the first she would have been raised to thirty had she remained. Would you care to start at twenty, with every assurance of an increase as soon as you are familiar with our work?"

Nine dollars a week was the largest wage June had ever received since she left Farris's, and that for but a single week in a temporary position. Would she accept twenty? She tried not to look too eager. With difficulty she seemed to hesitate, as though weighing in her mind the possibilities of the future against the present small pittance that had been offered her. Mr. Stickler eyed her steadily.

"The hours are not bad," he commenced.

"I do not care anything about the hours," she replied.

Mr. Stickler had it on his tongue's end to raise it to twenty-five — there were few girls applying for positions who did not ask about the hours at the first opportunity they had. Here was an exceptionally rapid and accurate stenographer who cared nothing about hours — she was indeed a find; and further, she was the finest-looking girl be had ever seen in his life. But before he had an opportunity June spoke.

"I think that will be satisfactory," she said. "When shall you want me?"

"When can you come?"

"Any time."

"Eight-thirty to-morrow morning."

"Thank you," said June. "I'll be here promptly. Good day."

"Good day, Miss Lathrop."

In the reception hall the furtive-eyed office-boy shot a keen glance at the young woman through half-closed lids as he looked up from some loose, printed sheets over which he had been bent in close study. He saw her glance at the name upon the door, which was now visible to her as she approached the doorway. He saw her give a sudden start and pale as though she had seen a dead man. Her hands went suddenly to her breast as she stood wide-eyed, gazing in horror at the neat, black lettering of the name.

Then she caught the boy's eyes upon her, and with a little effort she regained her composure and walked calmly from the office.

"John Secor & Co.!" she murmured to herself. "My God, I can never do it!"

But she did, and the next morning found her at work in the mahogany-furnished inner office of John Secor & Co. The girl could not recall that she had spent such another night of indecision and anguish for many a long month, until, with the close approach of dawn, she had determined to stifle the sorrow and loathing that thought of constant employment in that office induced, and take the position.

The twenty dollars a week meant to her, possibly, life itself, as well as the means of pursuing the straight and narrow path upon which a young man's smile had set her feet. She often wondered about him and if she should ever see him again. Some day she would like to thank him, she felt, for what he had done for her. Doubtless he had forgotten both her and the incident — she rather hoped that he had.

With her first week's pay, June partially repaid Eddie the Dip the money he had loaned her. For this purpose she met him at the little joint around the corner where one can feed up swell on two bits. Eddie was apparently as delighted with June's success as she herself, and that his pleasure was sincere was evidenced by the genuine disinclination he showed to accept a return of his money. But the girl insisted, and at last Eddie took the bills reluctantly.

In the far corner of the dingy restaurant a heavy man sat alone at a little table. He had been buried in an evening paper as the two had entered, so had not noticed them. When finally he looked up, running his shrewd eyes quickly about the room, he recognized Eddie the Dip, who sat facing him upon the farther side of the eating-place, near the cashier's desk.

No changed expression marked his recognition. Immediately he resumed his paper, turning in his chair so that while appearing to be reading he might surreptitiously watch the newcomers through the fly-specked mirror that circled the room above the wainscot. He had no further interest in them than that of semiofficial curiosity, and having recognized the man, he wished to discover the identity of his companion.

It was not until the two rose to leave that the girl turned her head so that the man in the far corner caught a view of her features. At sight of them he pursed his lips into a silent whistle of surprise; then Eddie the Dip paid the checks and the two passed out into the brilliantly lighted street.

The man at the table drew a note-book from his pocket, and with a stub of pencil wrote, laboriously, two names, the date, the hour, and the place; then he resumed the demolition of a large platter of "ham and."

Outside the restaurant Eddie bade June good night.

"You run along now, kid," he said.

"It wouldn't help you none to be seen with me."

The girl objected, though she knew well the truth of his statement. He alone in all the great city had evinced disinterested friendship in her and had given her real and substantial aid when she most needed it. Her sense of gratitude and loyalty was strong, and she would rather have missed almost anything than to have hurt the young man's feelings.

Doubtless Eddie guessed the truth of her sentiments; for he was firm in his insistence that she "run along home."

"You've been so good to me, Eddie," she said, "I —"

"Forget it," admonished the Dip.

"What's money for, anyway?"

"It is not the money I was thinking about," she replied, "though, of course, I could have done nothing without it — it's that you have been willing to believe that I wanted to be on the square — that I could be, and were willing to help me without" — she hesitated — "without expecting anything in return."

"Have I ever done anything to you, Mag," he asked with a laugh, "that gives you any license to class me with them Commonwealth Avenue or Lake Shore Drive guys?"

The following Monday morning June sat at her desk in the little office just outside that of the president of John Secor & Co. Ten days had passed since she commenced work there, and under the careful tutorage of Miss Smith and Mr. Stickler she had progressed rapidly in the assimilation of the details of her work.

Ogden Secor, the president of the company, she had not seen, as his return from New York had been delayed. She found herself wondering what he might look like, and if she should be able to continue in his employ after he returned. Now it was not quite so bad, for he was just a name; but when she should be compelled to come into daily contact with him, sit for hours, perhaps, close beside him as he dictated, would it not be very different and very terrible? The girl shuddered.

It was ten o'clock when Mr. Stickler opened the door from the president's office and called her. As Mr. Stickler often had given her work in this office before, she gathered up her note-book and pencil as she replied to his summons.

Somehow she did not like Mr. Stickler particularly.

He had a way of looking at her out of his fishy eyes that fell little short of being insultingly suggestive. When Mr. Secor returned she knew that she would be released from this distasteful ogling — unless Mr. Secor chanced to be of the same brand.

This, however, she doubted; for since her entrance into the world of business the girl had learned that the great majority of office men accord the same respect to their female coworkers — as they do to their own sisters. That there were exceptions she had also discovered.

At the door Mr. Stickler met her.

"Come in," he said, "Mr. Secor has returned; I wish to introduce you to him."

June felt suddenly all cold. She had known that this must come some time, but to that very instant she had not dreamed how terribly she dreaded the ordeal. Her heart seemed to go dead within her, and it was with difficulty that she raised her eyes to the face of the man who had risen courteously at her entrance. That she knew he had never before set eyes upon her did not lighten her burden of apprehension — it seemed that he must read the tragic truth that ran screaming through her brain.

And then at last she looked at him — the pleasant, honest smile; the cordial, outstretched hand. From cold she went hot. Could such a frightful contretemps actually occur in real life?

The man before her — her employer — was the young man whose kindly words had set her upon the road of righteousness! Would he remember her?

Chapter VIII

SAMMY THE SLEUTH

Ogden Secor did not recognize June Lathrop as Maggie Lynch, the girl from Farris's, and it was with relief that almost found expression in an audible sigh that the girl returned to her desk in her own office.

Here she surprised the lank and somber office-boy, Sammy, in the act of closing one of the drawers of her desk.

"What do you want, Sammy?" she asked pleasantly.

The youth went from white to red, and from red to scarlet. He stammered and coughed — trying to frame an apology, until June, from mild wonderment, became keenly suspicious.

"I'm awfully sorry, Miss Lathrop," he managed to get out at last. "I didn't mean any harm — I was only practicing."

"Practicing?" exclaimed the girl. "Practicing what?"

"I suppose," said Sammy, "that I'll have to tell you now; but I didn't want any one to know until I had graduated and got a position with Pinkerton."

"Pinkerton?" questioned June, still at a loss to make head or tail of what the youth was leading to. "What has practicing or Pinkerton to do with searching my desk surreptitiously? It was a very ungentlemanly thing to do, Sammy, and I really ought to tell Mr. Stickler about it."

"Oh, please don't do that," wailed Sammy. "Please don't and I'll tell you all about it."

"All right," said June, "now tell me."

"You see," said Sammy nervously, "I'm taking a correspondence course in a detective school, and a part of each lesson is to put into practice what I have learned in former lessons. Just now I was practicing searching a burglar's flat. Almost every day I practice shadowing."

"Shadowing?" exclaimed June. "What is shadowing? How do you do it?"

"Oh, it's easy," replied Sammy, his confidence returning as he discovered that June appeared to have forgiven the liberties he had taken with her desk.

"You see," he continued, "a detective has to be able to follow a suspect all over without being seen himself. I practice on lots of people — Mr. Stickler, Mr. Secor, Miss Smith, and the rest of them. When they go to lunch I shadow them, a different one nearly every noon. Friday I shadowed you — right into the Lunch Club on Wabash Avenue, and ate at a table behind you, and followed you back to the office and you never got onto me at all."

"Ugh!" shivered June. "How uncanny. Don't you ever dare shadow me again Sammy — promise me," and Sammy promised.

After the new stenographer had left his office, Ogden Secor tried to recall where he had known her before. He was positive that her face was familiar, and connected with some event in his life that was none too pleasant; but try as he would he could not place the girl. At last he dropped the matter from his mind.

For several months thereafter the routine of June's new life ran on smoothly and uninterruptedly. She saved the major portion of her salary, and once more met Eddie the Dip in the little restaurant that she might pay him the balance of the money she owed him.

Daily association with the life of the office of John Secor & Co. and its president eventually dulled the first revulsion she had experienced at thought of taking employment there. She found Ogden Secor all that she had grown to believe him since the day that he had come into her life from out of the grand jury room.

Of Mr. Stickler she grew more and more suspicious. There was no tangible overt act upon his part on which she could put her finger; nevertheless, she could have sworn, after a month of him, that he was a "hunter" without the nerve to hunt. He was, she grew sure, the sort that would take advantage of her first misstep to snare her, and so, without fearing him, she watched him and herself lest he might find some pretext upon which to make an initial advance toward her.

With the exception of Sammy, the office force was most uninteresting to any one outside themselves. Sammy was a never-ending source of joy to her now that she understood the motives which prompted his stealthy, catlike tread, his furtive glances, and his highly melodramatic appearances from directions in which one would least expect him to materialize.

As June never laughed at him — openly — he took a great liking to her, coming to her with his new lessons, with his hopes and his aspirations. His one and only ambition was to become a Pinkerton man, and he fully believed that once armed with the diploma of the correspondence school to which he paid half his weekly salary, it would be simply a matter of presenting it to the head of the detective agency to insure him an open-armed reception and an immediate appointment — didn't the prospectus of the school say so almost in so many words?

So secure had June grown to feel in the belief that her old life was absolutely dead and forgotten, and that Ogden Secor would never know that his private stenographer had been an inmate of Abe Farris's, that the shock of an occurrence through which she had to pass four months after taking the position all but unnerved her.

There was a caller in Secor's office, and as the buzzer upon June's desk sounded she took up her note-book and pencil to respond as she was called upon to do a dozen times in a day.

Scarce had she entered the inner office, however, than her heart seemed to cease its beating. Facing her, and looking squarely into her eyes as she passed through the doorway, sat the Rev. Theodore Pursen.

A look of half-recognition lighted his expression at sight of her. Instantly June jumped to the conclusion that he had come there to expose her but she managed to hold herself under perfect control as she advanced across the room to Secor's side, nor did she even, by a second glance at the visitor's face, betray the fact that she recalled ever having seen him before.

Secor handed her a memorandum.

"Make out a check," he said, "for this amount to the order of the Society for the Uplift of Erring Women."

June took the slip of paper and returned to her own office.

"Your secretary's face is quite familiar to me," remarked Pursen, after the girl had closed the door.

"Yes?" queried Secor politely, and uninterestedly. As a matter of fact, he was interested in nothing much that interested the Rev. Mr. Pursen — other than Sophia Welles.

"I am quite sure that I know her, but I cannot place her," continued Mr. Pursen. "Possibly her name might recall her to me."

"Her name is Lathrop," replied Secor.

Pursen shook his head. "I must be mistaken after all," he said, "I never knew any one of that name," and then June returned with the check.

For several days she was in a state of nervous apprehension, momentarily expecting a summons from either Mr. Secor or Mr. Stickler that would close her career with John Secor & Co.; but why she should dread discharge she could not guess, for she no longer felt a single doubt but that she should always be able to find pleasant and lucrative employment.

As a matter of fact, she finally decided, it was not so much discharge she feared, as that Ogden Secor should know her for what she once had been. The thought sent her white with terror, and with it came another thought — how much did her daily contact with Ogden Secor mean to her more than she had even faintly suspected?

Never before had this idea impinged upon her thoughts. She tried to thrust it from her. It was horrible. How horrible only she could guess; and yet, once fastened upon her, it clung tenaciously, a mighty load upon her conscience — a veritable Old Man of the Sea — so that she dreaded coming into Secor's presence for fear he might guess not only her secret, but as well the awful truth which made it the hideous thing it was.

Weeks rolled by. September came. June was once more lulled into a feeling of security. Secor was in New York on business. Sammy had been diligently practicing his lesson on thieves' jargon upon June until, convulsed with laughter, she had sent him back to his desk in the outer office.

Two rings of her buzzer called her to Mr. Stickler's desk. That fateful buzzer! Since the day that it had summoned her into the Rev. Theodore Pursen's presence she had never heard it without an inward shudder. To her relief she found that Mr. Stickler wished her merely upon an unimportant matter of detail. As he talked, Sammy entered, lynx-eyed and pussy-footed — Sammy could not cross the outer office, even to the water-cooler, without assuming a Hawkshawian gait that would have turned that worthy sleuth green with envy could he have seen it.

"Mr. Stickler!" he whispered, "two harness bulls are looking for you."

"Harness bulls!" exclaimed Stickler.

"What are harness bulls, Sammy?"

"Harness bulls," quoted Sammy from his recent lesson on criminal slang, "are policemen in uniform."

The sudden sickly pallor which overspread the face of the office manager did not pass unnoticed by either June or Sammy.

"Did they say what they wanted of me?" asked Mr. Stickler, controlling his voice with an effort.

Sammy lowered his own to a mysterious whisper. "They want you," he said, "to buy some tickets to the annual policemen's benefit at the Auditorium."

"Show them in," commanded Mr. Stickler in evident relief — even the best of men are often obsessed with an inexplicable terror of the minions of the law.

"That is all, Miss Lathrop," he added, turning toward June. "You may go."

As the girl left Mr. Stickler's office to cross the outer room to her own she saw two burly officers trailing in the wake of a suddenly metamorphosed Sammy. The youth walked with devilish swagger and outruffed chest. In his mind's eye Sammy was leading his trusty bluecoats to the arrest of a gang of counterfeiters whom he had tracked to their bidden lair.

As June passed the three she glanced casually into the faces of the policemen, and as her eyes met those of one of them it required every ounce of her self-control to hide both her surprise and terror.

It was Doarty.

A very suave and gracious Mr. Stickler laughed and chatted with the two policemen, purchased ten tickets to the benefit with John Secor & Co.'s money, and passed out a handful of John Secor & Co.'s cigars. As the two were about to leave, one of them turned to Mr. Stickler.

"How long have you had Maggie Lynch in your employ?" he asked.

"Maggie Lynch?" repeated Mr. Stickler. "We have no one by that name on our pay-roll."

"Well, then," said Mr. Doarty, "the young woman who came out of your office just before we came in?"

"Oh," said Mr. Stickler, "that is Miss Lathrop — Mr. Secor's private stenographer."

"Do you know anything about her?" asked Mr. Doarty, "or don't you want to?"

"Why, she seems to be all right," said Mr. Stickler. "But we know nothing about her other than that she had satisfactory references from former employers."

"Did she bring one from Abe Farris?" asked Doarty with a grin.

"Abe Farris?" exclaimed Mr. Stickler, and there was a little choking sound in his voice that entirely escaped the wily Mr. Doarty.

"Sure," said he, and then he leaned down and whispered into Mr. Stickler's ear for a moment. "— and," he concluded, "I just thought that maybe Mr. Secor might like to know the training his private secretary has had in the past — you'd better keep an eye on her.

Good day, and much obliged to you for taking those tickets."

It was not until nearly five o'clock that June's buzzer rang again, summoning her to Mr. Stickler's office. Already the force in the outer office was preparing to depart for the day. Mr. Stickler wished to dictate an "important letter," though to June, after he had commenced it it seemed rather too trivial for an overtime epistle.

For fifteen minutes Mr. Stickler dragged out his monotonous dictation. Then he rose and went to the door of his office. All had departed — the office was empty. He returned to his desk.

"Miss Lathrop," he said, "I have always liked you — in fact, I have grown very fond of you since you have been with us. I have been thinking that I must ask Mr. Secor to increase your salary; but before I do so I should like to feel that we are good friends — very good friends indeed, for only in connection with the most harmonious relations may we work together to the best advantage."

June was at a loss to guess what the man might be driving at. All she knew was that she did not like the sly expression of his little, close-set eyes, or the familiar manner in which he was hitching his chair closer to hers.

"I am afraid that I do not quite understand you," she said, her tone respectful, but cold and keen as a razor edge.

"I mean," said Mr. Stickler, "that I would like to see more of you outside of business hours — it will mean a lot to you in the way of advancement," he hastened to add as be saw the steely glitter that leaped to her eyes at his words.

June Lathrop rose. Mr. Stickler realized that never before had be seen any one quite so majestic, or quite so beautiful.

"Fortunately," she said, "Mr. Secor will return to-morrow. Otherwise I should leave at once. I shall not work another day in the same office with you, and to-morrow I shall give you an hour after Mr. Secor returns to tell him precisely what has passed between us in this office, then I shall go to him with my resignation and tell him myself."

Mr. Stickler went white with fear. He knew that the girl would do just what she threatened — unless — He glared at her and caught at the one straw that could save him.

"What else will you tell him?" he asked. "What else will Maggie Lynch tell Mr. Ogden Secor?"

It was June's turn to pale. Stickler saw the color leave her face and took advantage of the point in his favor.

"Come," he said, "be a good fellow. I don't want to be hard on you, and I'll forget all I know about Maggie Lynch and her job at Abe Farris's if you'll treat me right. Let's forget we've had any unpleasantness. We'll go over to the Bismarck and have a bite to eat and talk it over. Come on, little one, be a sport!"

The sneer on the girl's lip was sufficient reply to Mr. Stickler's suggestion. As she turned her back upon him and moved toward the door he sprang to his feet.

"Very well," he shouted, "I'll teach you. You're fired — do you understand? You're fired. I won't have any fast woman in this office, and if you show your face around here again I'll have Officer Doarty waiting for you."

June made no reply. Quietly she gathered up her personal belongings and left the office. When she had gone, Mr. Stickler banged to the office door and strode angrily toward the elevators.

No sooner had he left than a very pale and shaky Sammy emerged from beneath the sanitary filing-case in Mr. Stickler's office. He was "frightened stiff"; but with a grim determination that was upborne by a glorious enthusiasm he set forth to "shadow" Mr. Stickler.

Chapter IX

"UNCLEAN-UNCLEAN!"

Ogden Secor, stopping over at South Bend on his return from New York, arrived in town late in the evening of the day that had witnessed June's discharge. His chauffeur met him at the Lake Shore station, and together they drove down Jackson Boulevard to Michigan Avenue.

As the car swung to the north into the broad thoroughfare along the lake, Secor glanced up mechanically at the windows of his offices in the Railway Exchange, as he had done upon countless other occasions that he had passed the building.

To his surprise he saw that the rooms were lighted. It was past the hour that the janitor's assistants ordinarily cleaned his suite.

"Stickler," he thought. "He must be working on something of importance tonight. Pull up here, Jim!" to the chauffeur. "I'll run across to the office a minute before I go home."

For years Ogden Secor had entered his private office

through a doorway that opened directly off the main corridor. The custom had become so strong a habit that to-night he passed the main entrance of the well-lighted outer office, unlocked the door to his own unlighted office and entered, noiselessly, upon the soft, heavy rug that covered the floor.

A moment later he had crossed to the door that opened into the main office. Scarcely had he swung the door partially aside than his attitude of careless ease gave place to one of tense excitement. Directly across the office from him, with their backs toward him, two men bent to the combination of the great safe.

Secor's first impulse was to rush in upon them before they should damage the expensive and intricate mechanism of the lock with the charge of nitro-glycerin he imagined they were preparing to detonate; but as he took a step forward he suddenly realized that one of the men was turning the combination knob while the other read off the figures to him from a little slip of paper.

They had the combination. Where could they have obtained it? Only Stickler, Miss Lathrop and himself knew it. He looked at the men closely — he did not remember ever having seen either of them before.

Presently the door of the safe swung open, and Secor saw him who had manipulated the knob reach directly and without hesitation for the inner drawer that contained, ordinarily, a considerable quantity of negotiable paper. He waited to see no more.

Without a sound he ran quickly across the office, his only weapon, a light walking stick, swinging in his right hand. The first that either of the cracksmen knew that they were not alone in the office was the sudden and painful descent of the walking stick across be back of the head of one of them.

What happened after that happened rapidly — and almost noiselessly.

Two hours later Jim, the chauffeur, commenced to wonder if his employer had fallen asleep up there in his office. The North-East wind from off the lake was chill and penetrating. For another half hour Jim walked up and down the deserted sidewalk in a vain attempt to keep warm.

He had about decided to go up to the office and politely remind his employer that it would soon be time to breakfast when be heard a shot, apparently from the rear of the Railway Exchange across the street. The shot was immediately followed by hoarse shouts, and the sound of running men, and then another shot.

Almost immediately after the second shot Jim saw a man run out of Jackson Boulevard across Michigan Avenue toward Grant Park. He reached the center of the street only to crumple suddenly into a little heap. Behind him came a uniformed watchman, and presently a little crowd gathered.

"Caught him trying to make his getaway through the alley," explained the watchman to a city policeman who, attracted by the shots, had run over from Wabash Avenue. "There was another guy with him, but he broke in the opposite direction and got away. They'd been up to something in the Railway Exchange."

Instantly Jim thought of his employer and the unaccountably long stay he had been making in his office. Could these men have been the cause of his detention? Turning at the thought, he ran across the street and into the building.

At first the night elevator-man was disinclined to take him up; but when be explained who he was and what his fears, the man not only carried him aloft but accompanied him to the office of John Secor & Co.

Here they found the door to the main office ajar,

and within, upon the opposite side of the room in front of the open safe, the unconscious form of Ogden Secor. His head and face were covered with blood — even a casual glance proclaimed the fact that he had been terribly beaten. An ambulance from St. Luke's bore Ogden Secor to the hospital. It was late the following morning before the physicians would permit any one to enter his room, and then only after the greatest insistence on the part of their patient.

Miss Welles and the Rev. Mr. Pursen were the first to come. They were closely followed by Mr. Stickler, for whom Secor had sent. Mr. Stickler entered, white and shaky. It was quite evident that the accident to his employer had been a terrible shock to him.

Mr. Stickler had read an account of the daring robbery in his morning paper. He had known that Ogden Secor lay at St. Luke's hospital; but he had paced up and down his office for two hours before receiving Secor's summons to his bedside. Even then he had put off the ordeal for another half hour — surely Mr. Stickler's must have been a most sympathetic temperament, which shrank from the sight of the mangled countenance of his employer!

Before he started for the hospital he used the telephone.

"Is Officer Doarty there?" he asked, when he had obtained his connection.

"Hello, Mr. Doarty. You've read of what happened to Mr. Secor last night?

"And did you notice that the fellow they got — the one who was wounded — has been recognized as an habitué of Abe Farris's? Yes, and do you remember what you told me about that Lynch girl yesterday? Did you know she knew the combination to the safe? Sure; I thought of that right away.

"Yes, you bet. Wait a minute — I've got it here in my

file. Here it is — Calumet Avenue," and he gave a number, "she's rooming there. You'd better hurry. You'll be lucky if she hasn't left town already.

"What? Oh, I don't know yet — I've been too upset to figure it up, but it must have been close to twenty-five thousand dollars. No, bring her right to the hospital — I'll be there. All right. Good-by."

Half an hour later Mr. Stickler, on tiptoe and hat in hand, approached the bedside of his wounded chief. On his face was an expression of funereal sorrow.

"This is terrible," he murmured huskily.

"Well," said Secor with a wan smile, "they didn't quite get me, though it wasn't any fault of theirs that they didn't. Have you discovered just what they got away with, Stickler?"

Mr. Stickler hemmed and hawed. Evidently the answering of that question was one he dreaded.

"Why, I'm not quite sure yet, Mr. Secor," he said at last; "but there was, unfortunately, a considerable amount of negotiable securities as well as currency in the safe last night. You see, we had an exceptionally large pay roll on two big jobs for to-day, and we had drawn the cash yesterday because to-day, being Saturday, and a short day, we wanted to have everything in readiness to pay off promptly at noon."

"We've never been in the habit of doing that, Mr. Stickler," was Secor's only comment. "But come, how much did they get?"

"Close to twenty-five thousand dollars," whispered Mr. Stickler, and that it cost him an effort to say it was apparent to those about the bedside as well as to the injured man.

"But I think we'll get it all back," Mr. Stickler hastened to add. "They caught one of the fellows, and Doarty — of the detective bureau — telephoned me this morning that he expected to make an arrest within a few hours of the principal in the case."

"Good," exclaimed Secor. "But I cannot imagine who it could have been, or how they obtained the combination to the safe. Do you suspect any one in the office, Stickler?"

"I'd rather not say just yet, Mr. Secor," replied Stickler, "though I have my suspicions. When Doarty comes I think he will bring a big surprise along with him."

"It must have been through the connivance of some one in the office that they obtained the combination," said Miss Welles.

Mr. Pursen nodded. In the back of his brain an almost dead memory was struggling toward the light. Somehow it was inextricably confused with recollection of the face of Ogden Secor's stenographer, and a haunting, though vague, conviction that he had met the girl before and under no pleasant circumstances.

A moment later there came a knock upon the door. Mr. Pursen crossed the room and opened it, admitting a young woman and a large man. One glance at the latter would have been all sufficient to identify him to one city bred. There is something about the usual plain clothes man — whether his build, his carriage, or the way be wears his clothes, is difficult to say — that tags him almost as convincingly as would a uniform.

"Ah, Mr. Doarty, good morning," purred Mr. Pursen. He recognized June with an inclination of his head — very slight indeed.

The girl crossed directly to Secor's side.

"Oh, Mr. Secor," she exclaimed, her voice trembling with emotion. "It is awful. I had not seen a paper this morning and did not know until Mr. Doarty came for me, and told me."

She did not say what else Mr. Doarty had told her, principally by innuendo. Self was forgotten in the real affliction she felt at sight of her employer's pitiable condition. Secor looked up at her, his old, pleasant smile lighting his features.

"Oh, I guess it's not so bad," he said. "They ought to have me out of here in no time."

Miss Welles came closer to the bedside. Instinctively she guessed why Doarty had brought the girl here. Secor alone seemed to realize no connection between Mr. Stickler's recent hint and the coming of June Lathrop with the plain clothes man.

Doarty crossed the room to June's side, laying a heavy hand upon her arm.

"None of the soft stuff, Mag," he said roughly; "cut it out."

Secor looked up at the man in surprise, a frown crossing his face.

"What is the meaning of this?" he asked. "Miss Lathrop is my secretary. There has been nothing in her manner at all offensive — to me."

"I guess you don't know who she is, Mr. Secor," said Doarty. "Her name ain't Lathrop — it's Lynch, Maggie Lynch, and when I first seen her she was an inmate of Abe Farris's joint on Dearborn."

Secor looked at June questioningly. There was an expression of disbelief in his eyes. The girl dropped her own before his steady gaze.

The horror of it! If he could know — if Ogden Secor of all other men on earth could but know the truth — the truth that not even the shrewd Mr. Doarty had guessed.

At the voicing of the name Maggie Lynch, the Rev. Mr. Pursen stepped suddenly forward. The mists had been swept from his memory. As distinctly as it had been yesterday he recalled the humiliation that this girl had put upon him before the representatives of several of the city's great dailies. Even now he flushed at the memory of the keen shafts of ridicule that had resulted, and which had made the papers of the following day such frightful nightmares to him.

"Don't you remember her, Mr. Secor?" he cried. "She's the woman we tried so hard to help, and who ignored our godly efforts."

Mr. Secor remembered. He recalled the scene within the Grand jury room, and in the antechamber without. And he recalled many other things of which the others knew nothing — the intelligence and the loyalty of the girl since she had been in his employ. He remembered the several occasions upon which her tact or judgment had saved him from severe losses. He thought of the pleasure that he had always experienced in taking up the day's work since June Lathrop had been with him — something that he had never realized until that moment — and something of a dull ache oppressed his heart with the sudden knowledge that it was all over.

He had always thought of her merely as a part of the office force. He had never for a moment considered her in any other light than a faithful and almost flawless stenographer — nor did he now; yet there was a distinct sensation of personal loss accompanying the knowledge that he could now no longer employ her in so intimate a capacity as that of private secretary. His Puritanical prudery was too deeply ingrained to permit even a thought to the contrary.

To him, so far as his own personal association with such a person was concerned, the girl was as good as damned. He would as easily have considered consociation with a leper, though he would have been equally as willing to have helped either one or the other in any other way that did not require him to come into contact with them.

"What did you bring her here for?" he asked wearily. "There has been nothing in her deportment since she has been in my employ but what was entirely proper.

It seems unnecessary that she should be subjected to this humiliation."

"Her deportment *in the office* may have been all right," spoke up Mr. Doarty, "but we don't know so much what she was doin' with her time after office hours."

Mr. Stickler nodded his head portentously.

"You see, Mr. Secor," went on the plain-clothes man, "one of the guys that slugged you hangs out at Abe Farris's saloon, an' I seen Mag here, not so long ago, feedin' up in a beanery with another crook that hangs out at Farris's — Eddie the Dip's his name," and Doarty shot a sudden look in June's direction in time to see the quick intake of her breath in consternation and surprise.

"We got a drag-net out for Eddie now, an' when we get him I guess we'll have all three of 'em," concluded Mr. Doarty. He was very proud of this piece of police work of his.

"What has Miss Lathrop to do with it?" asked Secor. "She did not slug me."

"She knew the combination to your safe didn't she?" asked Doarty.

During the conversation June was aware that Miss Welles had drawn away from her, casting such a look of horror and disgust in her direction as might have withered her completely could looks wither.

Mr. Pursen, too, stood coldly aloof, while Stickler looked nervously down into Michigan Avenue from the window of the room, not once meeting the girl's eyes squarely.

Ogden Secor half raised himself upon his elbow. He looked straight into June Lathrop's eyes, and hers met his, as level and unflinching.

"Miss Lathrop," he said, in a very quiet voice, "are you in any way responsible for the rifling of the safe

— tell me the truth."

The girl's eyes never left his for a moment. Her reply was but a single word, delivered without emphasis, in a very ordinary tone.

"No," she said.

Secor sank back upon his pillow.

"That is all," he said, "you may go."

The doctor had just entered the room.

"You may all go!" he cried in a petulant voice. "I am surprised, Miss Castrol," to the nurse, "that you should have permitted this — come, get out, all of you."

Doarty came closer to the bed.

"You wish this woman held, of course?" he asked.

"Has any complaint been lodged against her?" asked Secor.

"Not yet."

"There will be none — you may let her go," said Secor.

Doarty looked his surprise, and seemed on the point of arguing, when the doctor placed a hand on his shoulder.

"Quick!" said the physician. "Get out of here, or I cannot be responsible for the recovery of this patient."

June took an impulsive step toward the injured man.

"How can I thank you for believing in me?" she cried.

With a weary sigh Ogden Secor turned away from her — he made no reply. The doctor led her to the door.

"Leave the room," he said.

Outside were those who had preceded her from the apartment. Mr. Pursen was the first to speak. He pointed toward the elevator.

"Leave the hospital at once," he said.

Her eyes filled with unshed tears, the girl walked quickly down the hall. At the elevator stood Doarty.

"You'd better beat it, Mag," he said.

"This town's too wicked for an innocent girl like

you," and from his tone she knew that he meant it — that much of it which warned her to leave the city.

Chapter X

"RATS DESERT —"

*F*or a long month Ogden Secor lay at St. Luke's. Surgeons pulled their whiskers, glaring owl-like at the patient the while they wondered why the deuce nature had not come to their rescue. At last she did — to some measure at least — and he was bundled off home, weak and broken.

They advised him to seek change and rest in a long ocean voyage; but he felt that his business, already long neglected, needed him. Not that he longer found the old keen delight in anticipation of strenuous coping with the storms and buffetings of the commercial world, but rather that habit drove him to it.

He found conditions in a frightful muddle. No one seemed to know what had been transpiring in the office — Stickler least of all. Secor did not deem it necessary to question Sammy — it had been better for him had he done so.

One of his first inquiries was for Miss Lathrop. Mr. Stickler looked at him in surprise.

"Why, I discharged her, Mr. Secor," he said. "You certainly cannot mean that you would have cared to continue her in our employ after learning the reputation she bore?"

"'Reputation'?" repeated Secor, "I do not quite grasp you, Mr. Stickler."

Mr. Stickler explained. It soon became evident to him that there was something radically wrong with his employer. There was a blank look of utter incomprehension upon Ogden Secor's face.

"It is odd," he said at last, "that I do not recall any of the incidents which you relate. You are quite sure, Stickler?"

"Quite sure, Sir."

As day succeeded day Ogden Secor realized more and more fully what an unusual secretary Miss Lathrop had been. He no longer mentioned her to Mr. Stickler, but he missed her very much, just the same. At times he recalled with a start the things that Stickler had told him about the girl's past, and then he would realize that after all it would have been impossible to have retained her. It was too bad, he thought; too bad — such secretaries as she were scarce.

As to Stickler's assertion that she had connived with the cracksmen, furnishing them the combination to the safe, Secor would not believe it.

Months rolled by. September came again. Long since Mr. Stickler had realized that his chief's memory was far from what it had been prior to the injuries he had received at the hands of the burglars. Ogden Secor, too, had guessed at something of the sort. He seemed to have lost his grasp. His usually alert mind was no longer equal to the emergencies that were constantly arising in his business.

Not only did he find it more and more difficult to close contracts, but those that he did obtain netted him losses now instead of the profits of the past. There was a leak somewhere, but Ogden Secor was not mentally fit to discover it.

Matters went from bad to worse. His losses on the year's work entailed the necessity of mortgaging the bulk of his real-estate holdings to complete a large public works contract in a neighboring city. Unable longer to concentrate his mind upon the work in hand, it ran completely away with him. Stickler assumed more and more the direction of it.

High prices were paid for inferior material, and for large amounts that were never delivered. Where the difference went the books of the corporation did not show, and if they had it is doubtful if Ogden Secor's waning mentality would have been able to understand that he was being persistently and systematically betrayed and robbed.

The final blow came when the engineers of the city for which the work was being done refused to accept it on the grounds that scarcely any of the material used was up to specifications. Coincidentally Mr. Stickler resigned his position with John Secor & Co., to accept the management of a stronger competitor.

An expensive lawsuit followed the refusal of the municipality, for which the work had been done, to pay the bill. In the end Secor lost. Bankruptcy proceedings followed, and on the first of the following February Ogden Secor found himself a ruined man — almost penniless, and broken as well in health and mentality.

With the exception of a worthless and barren farm in Idaho and a few articles of clothing, he had disposed of everything he possessed in an endeavor to meet the demands of his creditors. The farm, too, would have gone with the rest had he recalled the existence of it.

During the past few months of mental and nervous stress Secor had seen but little of Sophia Welles. He had not felt equal to the rounds of social activity which constituted her life, nor had he found her generously sympathetic.

Now that the end had come he sought her, hoping against hope that the ubiquitous Mr. Pursen would not be present. To his relief he found Sophia Welles alone.

She did not need the evidence of his tired and haggard face to realize the demand that might presently be made upon her sympathy and generosity — she had but just laid aside the noon edition of an afternoon paper in which she had perused the last of the rapidly dwindling references to a failure that had at first occupied a large part of the front pages of many editions. Sophia Welles knew at last that Ogden Secor was a hopelessly ruined man.

There was but one thing to do — she must forestall him.

"I am glad that you have come to-day, Ogden," she said, after a brief exchange of greetings. "For almost a year now I have had a great load weighing heavily upon my shoulders." — Miss Welles did not say upon her heart — " and I am only sorry that I did not speak of it long ago, for I can only too well realize the motives that may now be unjustly attributed to me in pressing the subject at this time of temporary financial trouble in which you find yourself.

"To be quite frank, I discovered long since that my affections were surely directing themselves toward another. I should have told you at once, but I was not sure at first, and I dreaded causing you useless pain."

She paused. Secor looked at her through dull eyes. It was evident that he was going to take it much harder than she had supposed.

It is true that not once since his accident had he spoken to her of their engagement. There had never been much in the way of sentimental exchanges between them, so that the absence of these had aroused little or no surprise in the girl's mind. She was glad now that it had been so, for it was going to make a difficult job much less difficult than it would otherwise have been.

Yet it was going to be hard enough — she could see that. She wondered why he didn't say something.

Finally he coughed — a slight flush mounting his pale face.

"I am quite sure, Sophia," he said, "that I shall always be most satisfied with what brings you the greatest happiness."

She noted the puzzled expression on his face, attributing it to a natural desire to learn who had supplanted him in her affections.

"I feel," she explained, "that we are not exactly suited to one another — our ideals are not the same. You do not find interest in that which interests me most, and so it seems to me that as there may never be any deep-rooted common interest between us that we should soon be most unhappy together."

The puzzled expression seemed to have been growing upon the handsome face of Mr. Ogden Secor.

"Yes," he breathed, "I fear that you are quite right."

"Mr. Pursen, on the contrary," went on Miss Welles, "feels precisely as I do upon the subjects that are closest to my heart — they are the same that are closest to his. In fact, Ogden, I am going to ask you to release me from my engagement to you."

Involuntarily Ogden Secor's mouth opened but whether in surprise or because of a terrible shock to his love and pride it would have been difficult to say. Miss Welles attributed it to the latter. At last he found words.

"My dear Sophia," he said, "you know perfectly well that if you love Mr. Pursen I shall be the last person on earth to stand in the way of your realizing to the full every happiness that may be found at his disposal. I congratulate you, Sophia — sincerely — and I beg that you will give no further thought to me other than as a friend and well-wisher."

"You are very generous, Ogden," she said, as she bade him good-by, glad that the ordeal was so easily over.

It would have been a much surprised Miss Welles could that young lady have read Ogden Secor's thoughts as he ran down the broad steps before her home and made his way to the nearest elevated station.

"And to think," thought hc, "that for over a year I have been engaged to Sophia Welles without once recalling the fact! Those cracksmen most assuredly cracked something belonging to Ogden Secor beside his safe."

It was with a feeling of relief and elation that he had not felt before for months that he strode along the street. Evidently the obligation of his engagement had been weighing upon him heavily through the medium of his subconsciousness without his having once objectively sensed other than an inexplicable call to duty that had drawn him to Sophia Welles when he gladly would have been elsewhere.

As he walked toward the elevated he tried to recall under what circumstances he had become engaged to Miss Welles. As he viewed the matter now it was difficult to realize that any possible contingency could have arisen that would have caused him to look with tender affection upon the cold and calculating Sophia.

The loss of his fortune affected Ogden Secor less than might have been expected. Possibly he did not fully realize the completeness of his financial ruin, or what it was bound to mean to him. In a way he felt principally a certain relief from the galling pressure and annoyances of the past bitter year. No longer was he weighted with burdensome responsibilities and grave apprehensions — the worst had happened. There was no further calamity possible — at least so he thought.

Vaguely he felt that he could again build up a fortune equal to that which was gone; but there was none of the old-time assurance and determination that had marked him in the past — it seemed quite impossible for him to concentrate his mind for a sufficient length of time upon the subject to formulate even the foundation of a well-considered plan.

He sought out old friends upon whose business acumen he might rely with the intention of talking over his plans with them, for at last, and the first time in his life, Ogden Secor felt unequal to the task of reasoning for himself, much less deciding in any matter of importance.

The first man to whom he went was the president of a bank of which Secor was still a director, and with which he had transacted the bulk of his banking business. The president was an old personal friend, a man of about Secor's own age, a member of the same clubs and the same set. Heretofore he had been wont to drop whatever had been engaging him and come into the anteroom to greet Secor whenever he had chanced to call. To-day the caller waited thirty minutes before the bank president appeared.

"Well, Secor," he said, "what can I do for you?" Heretofore it had always been "Ogden." There was an unquestionable air of haste in his manner, too; nor did he take Mr. Secor familiarly by the arm and drag him into his luxurious private office as formerly. It was just: "Well, Secor, what can I do for you?"

Those who are congenitally inefficient are prone to sensitiveness, and the same is often true of men who, through illness or preposterous circumstance, find themselves temporarily unfit to cope with the stern demands of modern success building. Supersensitiveness ofttimes begets a preternatural and almost uncanny ability to sense the secret motives underlying the acts of others.

Ogden Secor had never been over-sensitive. Until now he had not appreciated the fact that there could possibly be any material difference in the Ogden Secor of yesterday and the Ogden Secor of to-day. He had never gaged men by their bank accounts, so it is not strange that he should have been unsuspecting that any might have gaged him by such a standard.

The words and manner of the bank president, however, awoke him violently and painfully, for Ogden Secor was now, whatever he might have been in the past, an inefficient, and, accordingly, a supersensitive.

"There is nothing that you can do for me, Norton," he said. "I just dropped in for a chat. You're busy, though, and I won't detain you." He turned to go.

"I *am* mighty busy to-day," replied the bank president, a trifle more cordially. "Come in again some time, won't you?"

"Thanks," replied Secor.

When he reached the street he found himself cold all over — cold with a heart-coldness with which the bleak February northeaster had nothing to do. He did not venture to call upon another friend. Instead he dropped into a bar on La Salle Street and took a stiff drink of whisky. It was the first time he had done that for a longer time than he could recall.

The drink warmed him, sending an intoxicating, if artificial, renewal of hope and confidence surging through him. He took another.

There was a genial stranger drinking alone at the same bar. He commented upon the severity of the storm. Ogden Secor, friends with all the world now, entered into conversation with him.

"Wish I was back in Idaho," remarked the stranger, "where I could get thawed out and see that the sun was doing business at the same old stand."

Idaho! It awakened something in Secor's memory.

"I thought that it was usually pretty cold there," he said.

"Not where I come from," replied the stranger. "I got a little fruit-ranch down in the South-Western corner of the State. Greatest little climate in the world, sir; never gets anywheres near zero; and sunshine! Why, man, you ain't got a bowin' acquaintance with old Sol back here. Three hundred and sixty days of sunshine out of every three hundred and sixty-five."

Secor smiled. "You remind me of the boosters of sunny southern California," he laughed.

"Don't," said the Idahoan, raising a deprecating hand. "What *I'm* tellin' you is the truth."

"What part of Idaho did you say you are from?" asked Secor.

"'Bout ten miles south of Goliath. Goliath's a division headquarters on the Short Line."

"Goliath," repeated Secor. "Why, I've got a ranch around there somewhere myself — took it on a trade years ago and forgot all about it. One hundred and sixty acres, I think it was."

"Sort o' funny for a man to forget a hundred-and-sixty-acre ranch," remarked the stranger a bit skeptically.

During the following week Ogden Secor drank a great deal more than was good for him, or for any man. Several times he met old acquaintances on the streets. Ever eager now to discover changes in the attitude of former friends, he was quick to note the seeming coldness of their greetings, and the remarkable stress of unprecedented business which invariably hurried them along.

After each encounter he sought the nearest bar. His mind was much occupied with thoughts of his forgotten ranch, and when a summons to his attorneys' offices revealed the fact that the final settlement with his creditors would leave him with several hundred dollars of unexpected wealth, he obtained an advance from them, purchased a ticket for Goliath, Idaho, and shook the grimy snow of the Loop from his feet — he hoped forever.

Chapter XI

A MATTER OF MEMORY

*F*rom La Salle Street to Goliath Idaho, is ordinarily a matter of some two days' travel; but it required the best part of a year for Ogden Secor to perform the journey.

On the train he had become acquainted with an alert and plausible stranger who owned a gold mine in the mountains north of Ketchum. All that was needed for development was a few hundred dollars' worth of machinery and flumes — then it would make its owners fabulously wealthy.

By the time the train reached Shoshone, Ogdon Secor was inoculated with the insidious virus of gold-fever — that mad malady which races white-hot through the veins of its victims, distorting every mental image and precluding the sane functioning of the powers of reason.

In possession of all his faculties at their best, Secor could never have been trapped so easily; but what with weakened mental and physical powers — the result, primarily, of the work of the cracksmen, and later of the effects of alcohol, he fell an easy prey to the highly imaginative enthusiasm of his new acquaintance.

And so it befell that he left the train at Shoshone, and in company with the owner of the gold mine, boarded another for Ketchum, the northern terminus of the branch line.

Ketchum is, or at that time was, a squalid wreck of a place; but, like every other settlement of its stamp it boasted several saloons. To one of these the mine-owner led his victim. Here they discussed ways, means, and barbed-wire whisky until Secor passed over the few hundred dollars remaining to him that his new partner might go forth and purchase the necessary machinery and the outfit that was to transport it and them North into the mountains on the morrow.

Secor, waiting, drank with the proprietor, with the loungers about the place, and with others who drifted in scenting whisky at another's expense.

Night came, and still the mine-owner had not returned — nor did he ever.

Next morning Secor awoke, partially sobered, to a realization of the truth. He had been fleeced. He was friendless and all but penniless in a strange town; but, worst of all, his nerve was gone.

The year that followed was a hideous nightmare of regret and shame, the sole surcease from which was obtainable only through the stupefying medium of drink.

Often times he was hungry, for there was little chance to earn money in Ketchum. Again he did odd jobs about one or the other of the several saloons when a flash of his waning self pride or the growing desire for whisky goaded him to the earning of money.

Later he was given work as a clerk in the general store, his knowledge of accounting proving of value to the proprietor. This man, realizing that the continuous use of whisky would have no tendency to increase the value of his new clerk, employed him with the understanding that for six months he was to have but a small percentage of his wages weekly — just enough after the store closed Saturday night to permit of a mild orgy from which one might recover over Sunday and be fit for work on Monday.

At the termination of the six months, Secor demanded the balance of his accrued wage, and received it. Much to his employer's surprise, he failed to spend it immediately for drink. Instead, he did what he had been planning upon — took the first train south for Shoshone and Goliath.

In his mind was a determination to seek his farm and be thereafter independent of any employer. There was, too, the decision to stop drinking; but little did the man realize the hold the sickness had taken upon him.

Secor found Goliath a thriving town of three or four thousand inhabitants. His first inquiry, notwithstanding his good resolutions, was for a saloon, nor did he have any difficulty in locating several.

The tiresome journey from Ketchum had given him far too much leisure with only his own gloomy thoughts and vain regrets for company.

A little drink would do no harm — then he would stop. He would never touch it again; but just now his nerves required the stimulant. Then, too, was it not a well-known fact that in too sudden a cessation of the habit lay grave danger?

Ah, criminal fallacy! To you how many countless thousand graves owe their poor, miserable inmates!

And so it happened that at dusk it was a far from sober man who entered the Palace Lunch Room in time for the evening meal.

As he sat slouched down upon his stool, his befogged vision struggling with the blurred and scrawly purple of the mimeographed bill-of-fare, the girl waiting across the counter from him for his order could scarce conceal the disgust she felt at his slovenly and unkempt appearance. She could not see his face while his head was bent low above the greasy card, but she knew that it must be equally as repulsive as his soiled and disheveled apparel.

Who would have guessed that this object of the contempt of a cheap lunch-counter waitress in a far Western railroad town could have been the spotless Ogden Secor of two brief years ago?

Presently he looked up into the girl's face. At sight of his features she gave a little involuntary gasp, stepping back at the same time as though to avoid a blow.

"'Smatter?" asked Mr. Secor.

The girl eyed him intently for a moment, and then with a sigh of relief forced a smile to her white lips. He had not recognized her.

"Nothing," she said. "I'm taken that way occasionally."

"Heart?" asked Mr. Secor.

June Lathrop looked at Mr. Ogden Secor in silence for a moment.

"I wonder," she said, half to herself. "I wonder if it is?"

He gave his order and ate in silence, occasionally casting a furtive glance in the girl's direction. When she brought his dessert he asked where he might find a comfortable hotel.

"I only just arrived," he explained, "and am not familiar with the town." The meal had sobered him a bit, so that he could talk a trifle more coherently.

As he ate his pie June stood in front of him, talking. She told him where there was a room in a private family near by that he could probably get. She was filled with wonder at the change that had taken place in him. When his face was in repose the depth of sorrow that it revealed touched her heart. In vain she looked for the one-time radiant smile that had endeared Ogden Secor to many beside herself.

Could it be possible that this was the fastidious society and business man she had known but little more than two years since? It was incredible.

"Are you going to remain here?" she asked.

"I guess so," he replied. "I have a ranch around here somewhere. I've never seen it, but I'm going out tomorrow to have a look at it, and if it's all right I'll settle here and go to ranching. Much doing in that line?"

"Alfalfa and fruit ranches pay fairly well," she replied. "It depends, of course, on several things — soil, water rights and —" she hesitated — "the man who's ranching. Farming nowadays, you know, is something of an exact science. To be successful a man must understand that haphazard methods won't work."

"Can't a man learn?" he asked.

"Yes," she replied; "but even then he won't succeed if —" she hated to say it, but oh, how she hated to see him as he was — "but even then he won't succeed if he drinks."

Ogden Secor flushed. He was still far from having lost all self-respect. Without another word he paid his check and walked out of the lunch-room. It served him right, he thought, for having entered into familiar conversation with a waitress.

The following morning he engaged a buck-board and a driver for the trip to his ranch. A half hour's hunt through the records of the county clerk's office sufficed to locate his tract.

As he was driving through town he told his guide to stop in front of a saloon.

"We may get dry before the day's over," he explained with a grin to the more than willing native — it would never do to stop too suddenly.

As he stepped up to the bar and ordered a flask the words of the waitress came suddenly to his mind: "— but even then he won't succeed if he drinks." They seemed to take the keen edge off his appetite for whisky, but he pocketed the bottle and soon was jogging along through the stifling dust toward the only thing on earth that he might by any twist of the imagination call home.

As they drove along, Secor tried to picture the rolling meadow lands, the shady orchards, the broad, green fields of wheel-high, sweet-scented alfalfa of his ranch. Never before had he given this least valued of his possessions more than a passing thought, but now that it seemed to offer him a peaceful haven of rest and quiet, and utter seclusion from the world that he had known and come to hate, he viewed it through a mind's eye that glorified and idealized. He could scarce restrain his impatience with the slow, plodding team that wallowed now through sand to their fetlocks, and again labored upward toward the brow of a rough, lavastrewn bluff.

At last they came within sight of a broad, willow-fringed river. Low islands, dense thicketed, clove the strong, swift current with their sharp points. They might have been great, flat ships forging their silent way toward the distant mountains of the northland and whence the mighty river tumbled roaring downward for its thousand-mile journey to the waters of the lesser stream that steals its identity, onward to the sea.

All was greenish-gray or greenish-brown and all was sere and desolate and cold. Here and there little patches of half-melted snow lay in the shadows of the sagebrush that dotted the rolling flat beside the river.

Beyond, Secor could see a similar landscape upon the other shore.

"It is farther than I thought," he said to his guide.

"That's mostly the way in Idaho," replied the man.

Secor was wondering how they were to cross that mighty torrent, for it was evident that the ranch must be beyond the river — there were no signs of habitation, no rolling meadow lands, no shady orchards, no green alfalfa fields within his ken upon the river's hither side. He realized, of course, that the season precluded a full consummation of his dream, but there would at least be plenty to suggest the beauties of the Spring and Summer when they should come upon his home.

The guide drew rein upon a little knoll beside the river.

"Wanna get out?" he asked.

"What for?" questioned Secor.

"We're here."

Secor looked at him searchingly. Already the truth was leering at him with a contemptuous grin.

"Is this it?" he asked, nodding his head in a half swing that took in the surrounding desert.

"Yep," said the guide. "'Tain't much good. You ain't got no water."

Secor laughed — a weary, mirthless laugh.

"Oh," he said, "I think it's a pretty good place."

"Whafor?" asked the guide in surprise.

"To take a drink," said Secor, pulling the flask from his overcoat-pocket.

The guide grinned. "An' you don't need no water for that," he said.

"No," replied Secor, "water'd spoil it."

For weeks Secor frequented the Q. P. saloon at Goliath, emerging occasionally to eat and sleep. Every time he ate he was reminded of the waitress at the Palace Lunch Room, but he didn't go there. He wondered, when his mind was not entirely befogged by drink, why the girl should cling so tenaciously to his memory, and what cause there could be for the uncomfortable feeling that accompanied recollection of her warning — for warning it evidently had been.

One night Secor was sitting in a stud poker game. The gentleman next to him developed a crouching manner of inspecting his buried card, placing his eye on a level with the table and barely raising the corner of his own card. This permitted him to inspect Secor's buried card at the same time. A dozen hands were dealt before Secor discovered why he always won small pots and lost the large ones. Then he saw that his worthy opponent not only looked at Secor's buried card, but immediately thereafter passed obvious signals across the table to a crony upon the other side.

At the following deal Secor did not look at his buried card at all. He merely remained in on the strength of what he had in sight. From the corner of his eye he saw that the sly one was becoming nervous. Secor bad an ace and two deuces up — there was still one card to be dealt.

At the betting, Secor raised for the first time, then, purposely, he turned his head away from his cards and the man at his left to take a drink that stood at his right band. He guessed what would happen. When the drink was half way to his lips he turned suddenly to the left to discover the sly one in the act of raising his, Secor's, buried card to learn its identity.

Like a flash Secor wheeled, dashing his glass with its contents full in the face of the cheater. With the same move he came to his feet. The other whipped a revolver from beneath his coat. The balance of the players scattered, and the loungers in the saloon ran for the doorway or dived over the bar for the security its panels seemed to offer.

If Secor had been a foot further away from his antagonist he would doubtless have been killed. As it was his very proximity saved him. There is no easier weapon to parry at close range than a firearm. The slightest deviation of aim renders it harmless.

As the gun flashed beneath the electric light, Secor's left arm went up to parry it as if it had been a clenched right fist aimed at his jaw. The bullet passed harmlessly past him, and with the report of the exploding cartridge his own right landed heavily upon the point of the cheater's chin.

The man went backward over his chair, his head striking heavily upon a massive pottery spittoon. Then he lay perfectly still.

Ogden Secor stood with wide eyes gazing at the prostrate form of his antagonist — dazed. The bartender poked his head above the sheltering breastwork of the bar. Seeing that the shooting appeared to be over he emerged. His first act was to remove the gun from the nerveless fingers of the supine man. Then he turned toward Secor.

"Got a gun?" he asked.

Secor shook his head negatively. A moment later the players and the loungers returned to bend over the quiet form upon the floor. With them came the sheriff and a doctor. The former, after questioning the bartender, took Secor into custody, as several men carried the injured gambler into a back room.

All night Ogden Secor sat sleepless in his bare cell. He was very sober now, and the depths to which he had sunk were revealed to him in all their appalling horridness. It was unthinkable, and yet it was true — he, Ogden Secor, a participant in a drunken, saloon brawl! To-morrow, or as soon as they should release him, he would seek out the man he had struck and apologize to him, although he knew that the fellow deserved all that he had got.

He was sorry now that the bullet intended for him had not. found him. It would have been better so, and infinitely easier than to go on living the worthless, besotted life that he was surely headed for.

About eight o'clock in the morning the sheriff entered the corridor outside his cell.

"How's Thompson this morning?" asked Secor. Thompson was the name of the cheater.

"I guess he's comfortable," said the officer with a grin. "He ain't sent back for nothin'."

"Has he left town?" asked Secor.

"Yep," said the sheriff. "He's dead — you killed him."

Secor collapsed upon the hard bench at the side of his cell. He felt as though some mighty hand had struck him heavily over the heart. There was a look in his eyes that the sheriff had never seen in the eyes of another of the many killers he had arrested during his long years of service.

It was neither fear nor horror — the sheriff could not have interpreted it, for he knew not to what heights pride of name, of family, of station, birth, and breeding may lift a man above the sordid crimes, nor how awful is the plunge from such a pinnacle to the bottomless pit of shame which Ogden Secor's naked soul was plumbing that instant.

"You needn't take it hard," said the sheriff kindly. "You hit him in self-defense — there's half a dozen witnesses to that and to the fact that you wasn't armed. It was hittin' the spittoon with the back of his head that killed him. There ain't a jury in Idaho that'd find you guilty. You'd ought to have a medal, for of all the ornery cusses that ever struck Goliath that tin-horn was the most orneriest."

After the sheriff left him Ogden Secor sat with bowed head, his chin resting in his palms. He was surprised that the thought that he had killed a fellow man should not weigh more heavily upon him. It was the debauching degradation that had led up to the killing that caused him the most suffering.

The words of the waitress at the Palace Lunch Room came back to him once more: "— but even then he won't succeed if he drinks." Well, he wasn't succeeding in anything except getting rid of his little store of money.

What in the world was there for him to succeed at, anyway? he thought. If the ranch had been any good he would have pitched in there and worked hard. There he could have led a decent life, and earned a respectable living — he had no ambition for anything greater; but the sight of the arid sage-brush wilderness which had dispelled his dreams of fertile orchard, field, and meadow land, had so discouraged him that, since, he had been able to see no brighter ray than that which is reflected from the liquid fire that crossed the bar of the Q. P. in sparkling glasses.

As he sat buried in vain regrets and sorrowful memories, weighed down by thoughts of his utter friendlessness and loneliness, he became aware of the presence of someone approaching his cell along the short corridor.

Not sufficiently interested even to look up, he sat with eyes riveted upon the cold, gray cement of his prison floor. It was not until the footfalls halted before the bars of his cell that he raised his eyes. With a little start of surprise he came to his feet. Before him, smiling down into his face, stood the waitress of the Palace Lunch Room.

He looked at her inquiringly.

"I thought," she said, "that you might be lonesome here — that there might be something I could do for you."

If June Lathrop had required any reward for the generous impulse that had sent her to Secor's side in the time of his adversity she was amply repaid by the expression that lighted his face at her words. He almost choked as he attempted to reply.

"And I was just thinking," he said, "how absolutely friendless I am here. It is awfully good of you — I don't know how to thank you; but really you ought not to be here. I'm not — not the sort of person a decent girl should. know."

To what awful depths of self-abasement must Ogden Secor have sunk to voice such a sentiment as this! June felt the tears coming to her eyes.

"You mustn't say that," she said. "The sheriff told me all about it, and that you — it was in self-defense."

"It isn't that," said Secor. "It's that I was there at all — gambling in a saloon — and drunk. Drunk! I should have thought that would have killed whatever natural sympathy a woman might feel for a man who had killed another, even in self-defense. And," he continued, "do you remember the warning that you gave me the first day that I was in Goliath?"

"Yes," she said, "but I didn't think that you would."

"I have, a hundred times," he said. "And wondered why I should. I've wondered, too, what prompted you — did I seem as bad as that even then — or what was it?"

She did not dare tell him. He looked at her closely for a moment.

"Haven't I known you somewhere?" he asked.

She mustered all her courage. It was less on her own account that she dreaded telling him than on his. To be befriended by her might seem the last straw — the final depth below which there was no sinking.

"My name is Lathrop," she said; "June Lathrop."

Secor shook his head. "No," he said, "I don't know

you, but there is something mighty familiar about your face."

Chapter XII

JUST THREE WORDS

*T*he coroner's jury exonerated Secor. He was never brought to trial. For two weeks he remained in jail waiting the action of the grand jury. That body returned a no bill, and Ogden Secor stepped once more into the world of freedom.

During the period of his incarceration June had visited him daily. She felt, in a measure, a certain sense of obligation. This man, by a smile and a pleasant word, had set her feet back into the path of rectitude at a time when hope was gone from her life. She could do no less than exert what small influence she might wield to lead him from the path toward which he was straying.

She was glad that he had not remembered her, or at least that he had pretended that he did not. She was not sure which was the true explanation of his non-recognition. As yet she had not guessed the serious nature of the results that had followed his slugging at the hands of the cracksmen.

Between the noon and evening meals June had a couple of hours to herself, and it was at this period that she visited Secor in his cell. He came to look forward eagerly to her coming — except for a few of the Q. P.'s hangers-on, she was his only visitor.

It was June who brought him word of the grand jury's action. The kindly sheriff, meeting her at the jail's door, as he himself was bearing the news to the prisoner, told her that Secor was a free man, and that she might carry the cheering message to him.

"I reckon he'd rather hear it from them pretty lips, anyway," he added, winking knowingly.

June flushed. It had never occurred to her that any one might find foundation for imagining the existence of tender sentiments between herself and Ogden Secor in her daily visits to the prisoner. So it was with an emotion akin to diffidence that she approached his cell that day.

Secor received the news of his final exoneration without any show of elation. June looked at him in surprise.

"Doesn't it make you happy" she exclaimed. "Why, I wanted to throw up my hat and shout when the sheriff told me."

He shook his head. "Why should it make me happy?" he asked. "What am I coming out to? Who cares whether I am in or out?" And then at the hurt look which she could not hide, he exclaimed, regretfully: "Oh, I didn't mean that exactly — I know that you care, and it means everything to me to know that there is one good, kind heart in the world; but, Miss Lathrop, your generosity would go out the same to a yellow dog — but not your respect.

"You can't help being kind and sweet, for your soul is pure and true — I can read it in your eyes; but even that can't blind you to the bald and brutal fact of what

I am — a drunken bum."

The bitterness of his tone turned the girl cold.

"And what am I coming out to" he went on. "I'm coming out to the Q. P. — that'll be the first place I'll head for. There is no other place that I may go, and tonight I'll be drunk again."

She stretched her hand between the iron bars and laid her slim fingers on the man's arm. Her eyes were dim with tears as she raised them to his.

"Oh, don't," she pleaded, "please don't! You mustn't throw your life away. Remember who you are — what you have been — what you may be again. Oh, won't you promise me that you'll never touch it again?"

The tear-filled eyes, the pleading voice, the touch upon his arm, sent a sudden thrill through every fiber of Ogden Secor's being. Never before had he realized half the beauties of the girl's face and soul as revealed that instant as she pleaded with him for his own honor.

He forgot that he was Ogden Secor — that she was a waitress in a cheap lunchroom. Slowly his hand crept up until his fingers closed upon hers. He leaned forward close to the intervening bars. There was a light in his eyes that had never shone upon Sophia Weekes.

"June!" he whispered, his voice now husky with emotion. "I can stop — I can do anything for your sake. June, I I —"

Like a flash the girl snatched her hand from his. Her fingers flew across his lips as though to smother the word that he would have spoken — it seemed almost like a blow.

"*No!*" she fairly shouted. "Oh, God, you don't know what you are saying! Don't say it — don't think it. It is *too awful!*" and pressing her clenched hands to her face she turned and almost ran from the jail.

For a moment Secor stood as though stunned. He had seen the horror mirrored in the girl's eyes — and he had placed the only interpretation upon it that he could.

"God," he muttered as he sank to his hard bench, "have I sunk so low as that?"

A few minutes later he was released from jail. He did not hesitate. With long, eager strides he made straight for the Q. P.

For a month he scarce drew a sober breath. Then he landed in jail again — this time as a plain "drunk" — he had been picked up from the gutter by a town policeman.

June heard of it, and came to his cell early the next morning. He met her look almost defiantly, but at the pain and sorrow in her face his eyes wavered and fell.

"I shouldn't think you want to sully your name by coming to see the town drunkard," he said; and then, bitterly, "I'd have stopped for your sake even without your love. I don't blame you for that; but you needn't have been so disgusted with the thought that I loved you."

"You didn't think *that?*" she exclaimed.

"What else could I think? I read it in your expression."

"Oh, it wasn't that," she cried. "You must know that I couldn't come to see you, or want so to help you, if I felt that way!"

"Then what is the reason? Why can't I tell you that I love you, June?" he insisted. "Tell me."

"I can't," she said, "and you mustn't ask me to tell you."

She was close to the bars now, and again she laid her hand upon his.

"I would do anything on earth for you, Ogden," she said, "except let you love me. Why can't you let me help you to win back the biggest thing you have lost — your self-respect? The rest will be easy then, and when you have it once more you'll want to get down on your knees and thank June Lathrop that she wouldn't let you fall in love with a — waitress."

"Would it make you any happier?" he asked.

"It would make me happier than I had ever expected that I could be again."

"I'll try," he said, "for your sake; but how am I to begin — what is there for me to do?"

"Your ranch," she returned promptly. You told me that you had a ranch down near the river."

Secor laughed. "I went to see it when I first came out. It's nothing but an unfenced sage-bush desert. No water, no fences, no house — nothing."

"There's the river," she urged.

"And what can I do with the river?"

"With a shovel and a pan, you can get a living wage out of the gravel anywhere along the river," she answered. "And you can live clean and decent. You're making nothing here, and you're living like a hog."

Ogden Secor flushed. The words stung him, and because they stung, they did more to crystallize the good intentions that the girl's pleas had aroused than would further pleading, for they awoke with him the fast-dying flame of his self-respect.

"I'll do it, June," he said, "for your sake; but give me something to hope for, if I succeed. Tell me that you may then listen to what you won't listen to now."

"When you are back where you should be," she said, "I mean physically, morally, and mentally, you won't care to have a waitress hear you tell her that you love her."

"I'm not in love with a waitress, June; I've dared aspire to an angel."

The police magistrate before whom Secor was arraigned had acquired local celebrity through the success he had made of keeping Goliath fairly free of bums and hoboes. The sheriff and the constabulary worked with him. They arrested every undesirable stranger upon the streets, and the judge forthwith put them back upon the streets, padlocked to a long chain. There they worked out their sentences until, released, they shook the dust of Goliath from their feet, nor ever thereafter ventured within her limits.

To this good judge Mr. Ogden Secor looked like any other drunken bum that was hailed before him. There was, it is true, that about the cut of his disheveled clothes which proclaimed a one-time smartness; but this rather militated against the defendant, for in it the judge saw more sinister signs than mere worthlessness — Eastern crooks, he knew, were ofttimes smartly clothed, or the man might have stolen the apparel, which was more likely.

"Three days in the chain-gang," said the judge. "Call the next case."

Before those three awful days were over, Ogden Secor was more thoroughly sober than ever he had been in all his life — even in the days that he did not drink. He worked with eyes bent upon the ground, never once raising them. Through his mind ran four words — the words of hope and encouragement that June Lathrop had spoken: " There's the river." But now it was a grim and sinister interpretation that he put upon them.

"There's the river!" He could scarce wait for the knocking of his galling fetters from his ankle. "There's the river!" Yes, and there, too, lay forgetfulness of the hideous humiliation of these frightful days.

June Lathrop saw him in the chain-gang, as the motley crew worked upon the streets of Goliath. She turned her head away lest he should see that she had seen, and hurrying to her room, threw herself face down upon the bed, sobbing. Her tears were for him, for the hideous laceration of his pride that she could read in the bent head and the stooping shoulders. He had looked like an old man, tottering to his grave beneath a hopeless load of shame.

God, how it had hurt her! Yet by all the age-old traits that are ascribed to humanity she, of all others in the world, should have found sinister rejoicing in the suffering of this man. But instead, there came to her for the first time a realization of the one thing above all others that might make her life even more miserable than it had been — she loved Ogden Secor.

She knew now that she had always loved him — since that day that he had met her in the antechamber of the grand jury room. She saw now why she had set herself the task of reclaiming him. She saw, too, why she had experienced such horror at the thought of his voicing words of love to her — it was because she had loved him, and because in all the world of men and women, he and she had the least right to love one another.

When Secor's time in the chain-gang was up, June was waiting for him outside the jail.

Love had given her the power to read in the humiliation of the man she loved something of the stern resolve that had found lodgment in his mind. Intuitively she sensed what would be the first impulse of a proud man weakened by dissipation and bowed down by humiliation.

She had been a "down-and-outer" herself. She had been on the verge of the very thing she had guessed Secor to be contemplating — it had come after that terrible morning at St. Luke's — but the memory of Ogden Secor's kindness to her had stayed her hand.

Now she would repay him.

With head still bowed and eyes upon the ground he emerged from the jail. When June fell in beside him, he did not look up, though he knew that it was she —

who else was there in all the world who would be seen upon the public streets with him?

In silence they walked side by side through the little city, down the dusty road toward the cool shadows of the tree-bowered brook that winds along that pleasant valley.

Secor moved but with one thought in his mind — to get beyond the sight of his fellow men. They came at last to the brim of the little stream. There were no prying eyes about them.

June touched his hand gently where it hung at his side, and then her cool fingers closed upon his.

"Ogden," she whispered.

He turned dull eyes upon her, as though for the first time realizing her presence.

"What are you doing here?" he asked; and then, without waiting for her reply, went on: "And you walked at my side through the streets — through the hideous streets where I have worked with a chain upon my ankle, fastened to vagabonds and criminals, and to — to bums — to other bums like myself — drunken bums! Every one must have seen you — Oh, June, how could you have done it?"

His thoughts now were all for her. There could have been nothing better for his sick brain, nauseated with continual thinking of his own shame.

"I must have been mad to let you do it," he went on. "Your friends will jeer at you. They will link your name with that of Ogden Secor, the town drunkard —"

She clapped her hand over his lips.

"You mustn't say that!" she cried. "I won't let you say it! You are not that — you never could be that. You are making a mountain of a molehill. It is not the man who falls who receives the censure of his fellows; it's the man who falls and won't get up — who lies wallowing in the filth of his degradation. The world admires the man who can 'come back' — it hates a quitter.

"You have told me that you love me." She was speaking rapidly, as though everything in the world hinged upon the element of time. "You have asked me to love you. Do you expect me to love a *quitter?* You are thinking this minute of adding the final ignominy to your downfall; you are thinking this minute, Ogden Secor, of taking your own life. If I could love a quitter, do you think that I could love a — *coward?*"

Beneath the lash of her words, the man within him awakened. His shoulders straightened a bit. He looked her straight in the eyes for the first time that day. He was trying to fathom her interest in him. Presently he seemed to awaken; a sudden light dawned upon him. Hope lightened the lines of his tired and haggard face. Not for months had he looked so much like the Ogden Secor of the past.

He took the girl by the shoulders.

"June," he cried, "I have been trying to guess why you should have done for me all that you have done. There can be but one reason. You cannot deny it. Let me hear your lips speak what your acts have proclaimed. Tell me that you love me, June, and I can win back to any heights!"

She pushed him gently from her. Her heart ached to be pressed close in the arms of the man she loved; yet she knew that it could never be. If her love would save him, she had no right to deny it, though she knew that such an avowal could bring nothing but misery and shame to them both; there never could be any consummation of a love between Ogden Secor and June Lathrop.

"I could not deny it now," she said at last, "and if it will help you any to hear me say the thing I have no right to say, or that you have no right to hear, I can do it for your sake; but beyond the saying of it, Ogden, there can be nothing. That we must both understand. Why, I cannot tell you — I dare not. Do not ask me."

"It will be enough for now," he said, "to hear you say it. Afterward we shall find a way; love always does, you know."

And so she said the thing he wished to hear, nor never in all his life had words sounded sweeter to Ogden Secor than those three from the lips of the waitress from the Palace Lunch Room.

Chapter XIII

"FOR THE MURDER OF —"

*F*or a year Ogden Secor toiled at his lonely camp beside the big river.

His shovel and his pan and his crude rocker were his only companions. With the little money that had remained to him after his wasted days in Goliath he had purchased material and tools for the construction of a frail shack on his land close to his placer diggings, and had furnished it with such bare necessities as he could afford.

Once a week he walked the ten miles that lay between his camp and Goliath for a few hours with June Lathrop. These were red-letter days for them both — the sole bright spots in their lonely lives peopled by vain regrets.

At first lie had tried to wring from the girl an explanation of her refusal to listen to a suggestion of their marriage; but finding that the subject caused her only unhappiness, he desisted. The Q. P. knew him no more during these days, and the change that was wrought in him by abstinence and healthful, outdoor labor was little short of marvelous. He grew to take a keen pleasure in his physical fitness, and with renewed health of body came a return of his former mental efficiency — what the surgeons, tinkering with his hurt skull, had been unable to accomplish, nature did; slowly, it is true, but none the less effectively.

As his vigor of mind increased, his memory returned in part, so that he was constantly haunted by a growing conviction that somewhere, some place far from Goliath, he had known June Lathrop, and that she had been intimately associated with that other life that was once again taking concrete form in his recollections.

Not that he had ever entirely forgotten his past, for he had not. Rather, he recalled it as through a haze which confused and distorted details so that he was never quite sure of the true identity of what he saw back there in the years that were gone.

But after all else was plain the figure of the June Lathrop of the past still remained little else than an intangible blur. There was something needed to recall her more distinctly than his unaided memory could do — nor was that thing to be long wanting.

The gold that Secor washed from the gravel of the old river bar was barely sufficient to meet his daily needs. As a result his ranch — he always laughed as he referred to the bit of sage-brush desert as "my ranch" — was sold for taxes. The time was approaching when, if he would regain it, he must act; but having no money, he was forced to remain helpless as the time approached.

One day while he was in Goliath he mentioned the thing to June.

"Of course the land is not worth the taxes," he said; "but somehow I have grown attached to it — it's the only 'home' I have. I shall hate to see it go, but I'll be as well off, I suppose."

"Not worth the taxes?" she exclaimed. "Why, Ogden Secor, where have you been for the last six months? Didn't you know that the new government reclamation project is at last an assured fact, and that your land will jump from nothing an acre to something like a hundred dollars an acre overnight?"

Secor looked at her blankly.

"I didn't know it came as far down river as my holdings," he said.

"Why, your land is right in the center of it — there is every chance in the world that the new town will be located there, and if that happens you'll be wealthy."

He smiled ruefully.

"Not I," he said; "for I couldn't raise the money to redeem the ranch if my life depended on it."

"How much is necessary?" she asked.

He told her. The next day, Monday, she drew her savings from the bank and turned them over to Secor.

At first, when she had suggested this thing, he had refused flatly, but after talking with several men who were well posted, he had seen that there was no question but that the land would increase in value immensely and that he should be able to repay June in the near future.

The same day word came of the exact location of the proposed town — it brought definite information to the effect that a large portion of Secor's holdings would lie directly in the business center of the town, and the balance on the gentle rise back from the river that had been set apart for residential purposes.

June and Ogden were so elated they could scarcely contain themselves. Nothing would do but that they must celebrate with a dinner at the Short Line Hotel — the most pretentious hostelry of Goliath. At first June demurred, but Ogden was insistent, and so she asked for the afternoon and evening off.

They strolled together beside the little stream where he had wrung from her lips an avowal of the love she had no right to harbor for Ogden Secor. Once again he revived the subject that had long been taboo, urging her to forget whatever to him unfathomable scruples kept her from him; but she only shook her head sadly, and when he saw how unhappy it made her he tried to drop the subject, though he found it most difficult to drop.

As they approached the hotel where they were to hold their modest celebration the Limited from the East lay along the platform, up and down which the passengers were strolling. To reach the dining-room it was necessary to walk past a part of the long line of Pullmans and as they did so Secor was suddenly confronted by a trim little man with outstretched hand.

"My dear Secor," he exclaimed, "what in the world are you doing here? We have all wondered what could have become of you."

And then turning toward the open window of a drawing-room he called, "Oh, Sophia, see whom I have discovered!"

Sophia Welles Pursen looked from the window — she and the Rev. Mr. Pursen were on their bridal trip. She saw Ogden Secor and beside him she saw another whom she recognized. Coldly she barely inclined her head, turning away from the window immediately.

Then Mr. Pursen looked at Ogden Secor's companion for the first time. He, too, recognized her.

"My gracious!" he exclaimed. His eyes went wide in holy horror. "My gracious! Excuse me, Secor, but the train is about to start." And without a backward glance be hastened toward his car.

The sight of Sophia Welles and the Rev. Mr. Pursen, and the glances of contempt they had shot toward June

Lathrop, had done in an instant what months of vain attempt at recollection had failed to do. With the suddenness of an unexpected slap in the face there returned to Ogden Secor the memory of the last time he had seen these three together.

As clearly as if it had been but yesterday he saw the figures about his bed as he lay propped up upon his pillows at St. Luke's.

He saw Sophia Welles and the Rev. Mr. Pursen. He saw Stickler, nervous and unstrung, and he saw Doarty, his heavy hand upon the arm of the girl from Farris's.

Slowly a dull red crept across his face. He turned toward June. The look of misery in her eyes showed that she realized that memory had returned.

"Now you understand at last," she said in a dull voice.

He took her by the arm and led her into the dining-room. She scarce realized what she was doing when she permitted herself to go with him. He found a table in a corner, seating himself across from her.

"The cad," he said — " the dirty, little, hypocritical *cad!*"

She looked at him in astonishment.

"You mean —" she started.

"I mean Pursen."

"But he was right — he couldn't recognize me," she replied wearily. Then she rose from the table. "I'll go now," she said "I don't know why I came in here — I must have been — stunned. I knew that you would find out some day — but I didn't know that it would be so dreadfully terrible."

Her lips trembled.

He reached across the table and forced her gently back into her chair.

"The only terrible thing about it," he said, "is that there should be such people as the Rev. and Mrs.

Pursen in the world. That, and the fact that they have made you unhappy."

"You mean that you don't hate me, now that you remember?" she asked.

"I have guessed for a long time, June," he replied, "that there was something in your past life that you thought would make our marriage impossible if I knew of it. You have misjudged me. I do not care what you have been or what you have done. That is past — it can't be helped now, or undone. All I know is that I love you, and now that I know all there is to be known, there can be no further reason why you should hesitate longer."

The old smile lighted his face. "Oh, June," he said, "can't you see that it is only our love that counts? If *you* can forget what *I* have been — if you can forget the saloon brawls — if you can forget the chain-gang — what have you done that I may not forget? For you were but a young girl, while I was a strong man. Nothing that you may have been can exceed in ignominy the depth to which I sunk."

"You do not remember all, then," she said sadly. "You have forgotten what Doarty accused me of — giving the combination to the man who robbed the safe."

"I remember everything," he replied, "but I do not believe it — no, I do not want you even to deny it, for that would imply that I could believe it."

"I am glad that you don't believe it," she said, "for that, at least, was not true! But the rest is true — about Farris's."

He could not help wincing at that, for he was still a Puritan at heart.

"Let's not speak of it," he said. "It doesn't change my love for you. I am sorry that it had to be so, but it is, and we must make the best of it, just as we must make the best of the memory of what I became here in Goliath — the town drunkard. I want you, June, and now there is nothing more to keep you from me. Tell me, dear, that there is nothing more."

She was about to reply when a broad-shouldered man arose from a table behind them. As he approached June was the first to see his face. At sight of him she turned deathly pale — it was Doarty. He stepped to her side and laid his hand upon her shoulder.

"Well, Mag," he said, "I've had a devil of a time finding you; but I've got you at last."

Ogden Secor leaped to his feet.

"What does this mean?" he cried. "Who are you? What is it, June? What does he mean?"

Mr. Doarty did not recognize Mr. Ogden Secor, whom he had seen but once or twice and then under very different circumstances and in widely different apparel.

"It means, bo," said Mr. Doarty, "that your lady friend is under arrest for the murder of John Secor four years ago."

Chapter XIV

SOME LOOSE THREADS

*T*he case of the People *versus* June Lathrop, alias Maggie Lynch, came to trial in the old Criminal Court Building. Since her arrest June had persistently refused to see Ogden Secor, though he had repeatedly endeavored to have word with her. She felt that his desire to come to her was prompted solely by gratitude for her loyalty to him when their positions had been reversed — when he had been the prisoner.

How the case had come to be revived no one seemed able to explain. A scarehead morning newspaper had used it as an example of the immunity from punishment enjoyed by the powers of the underworld — showing how murder, even, might be perpetrated with perfect safety to the murderer. It hinted at police indifference — even at police complicity. No Secor millions longer influenced the placing of advertising contracts.

The police in self-defense explained that they had never ceased to work upon the case, and that they were already in possession of sufficient evidence to convict

— all they required was a little more time to locate the murderer. And then they got busy.

It happened that Doarty knew more about the almost forgotten details of the affair than any other officer on the force, so to Doarty was given the Herculean task of locating Maggie Lynch. Another officer was entrusted with the establishment of a motive for the crime and an investigation of the antecedents of Maggie Lynch.

The results of the efforts of these two sagacious policemen were fully apparent as the trial progressed.

At first it seemed that there would be neither lawyer nor witnesses for the defense, but at the eleventh hour both were forthcoming. Ogden Secor had seen to that, and there was presented the remarkable spectacle of a young man working tooth and nail in the building up of the defense of the woman charged with the murder of his uncle.

All that he knew at first was that she had been an inmate of the house where John Secor had dropped dead of heart disease. The State, to establish a motive brought a slender, gray-haired woman from a little village fifty miles south of the metropolis.

She was sprung as a surprise upon the defense, and as she was called to the witness chair from the antechamber, June Lathrop half rose from her chair — her lips parted and her face dead white.

The eyes of the little woman ran eagerly over the court-room. When they rested at last upon the face of the defendant, tears welled in them, and with a faint cry and outstretched arms she took a step toward June.

"My daughter!" she whispered. "Oh, my daughter!"

A bailiff laid his hand gently upon her arm and led her to the witness chair.

Her story was a simple one, and simply told. She related the incident of the first meeting of "John

Smith" and June Lathrop. Smith's automobile had stalled in front of the Lathrop homestead, and while the chauffeur tinkered, the master had come to the door asking for a drink of water. He had seen June, and almost from that instant his infatuation for the girl had been evident. Afterward he came often to the little village where the daughter and her widowed mother lived.

Finally he spoke of marriage. June had told her mother of it, and that she hesitated because of the great difference in their ages — she respected and admired John Smith, but she did not know that she loved him.

He brought her beautiful presents, and there were promises of a life of luxury and ease — something the girl had never known, for her father had died when she was a baby, and the mother had been able to eke out but a bare existence since. It had been the promise of ease and plenty for her mother's declining years that had finally influenced June to give a reluctant "yes."

They had been married quietly by a justice of the peace, and had been driven directly to town in Smith's machine.

The former Secor chauffeur established the identity of Smith as John Secor. He distinctly recalled their first visit to the Lathrop home, and almost weekly trips to the little town thereafter. He positively identified the defendant as the girl whom, with John Secor, he had driven from the Lathrop home to the city on the day of the wedding, at which he had been a witness.

"Where did you leave the couple after arriving here?" asked the State's attorney.

"At Abe Farris's place on Dearborn," replied the witness.

When June was called to the stand she corroborated all that had gone before. It seemed that a motive had been established.

"Did you know the nature of the place to which Mr. Smith took you at the time?" asked her attorney.

"I did not. He told me that it was a family hotel, and when, after we had been there a few days, I remarked on the strange actions of the other guests — their late hours, ribald songs, and evidences of intoxication, he laughed at me, saying that I must get used to the ways of a big city."

"Did you believe him?"

"Of course. I had never been away from home in my life. I knew absolutely nothing about the existence even of such places as that, or of the forms of vice and sin that were openly flaunted there. I was so ignorant of such things that I believed him when he told me that the men who came nightly to the place were the husbands of the women there. We had a room on the second floor, and though I heard much that passed in the house, I saw very little out of the way, as we kept closely to our room when we were in the place."

"When did you discover that your 'husband' already had a wife living, and that his name was John Secor and not John Smith?"

"About half an hour after he dropped dead in the hallway," she replied. "Abe Farris came to me and told me. He offered me a hundred dollars to keep still and pretend that I had never seen or heard of Mr. Secor. I didn't take the money. I was heartbroken and sick with horror and terror and shame. I wouldn't have told any one of my disgrace under any circumstances. Farris kept me there for two days longer, telling me that the police would arrest me if I went out. Finally I determined to leave, for at last I knew the whole truth of the sort of place I was in.

"Then Farris urged me to stay there and go to work for him. When I refused, he explained that I was already ruined, and even laughed when I told him that

I did not know that I was not legally married to Mr. Smith. 'You don't think for a minute that any one'll swallow that yarn, do you?' he asked. 'If you want to keep out of jail you'd better stay right here — you can't never be no worse off than you are now.'

"I began to feel that he was right, yet I insisted on leaving, and then he had my clothes taken from me, saying that I owed him money for board that Mr. Secor had not paid, and that he would not let me go until I paid him.

"I think that I must have been almost mad from grief and terror. I know that at last I grew not to care what became of me, and when Farris made me think that I could escape arrest only by remaining with him, I gave up, for the thought that my mother would learn the awful truth were I to be brought to trial was more than I could bear."

Farris testified that he had been the first to tell the girl that the man she thought her husband was the husband of another woman.

"When did you tell her this?" asked the attorney for the defense.

"Half or three-quarters of an hour after Mr. Secor died."

Afterward two reputable physicians testified that they had performed a post-mortem examination upon John Secor's body — that there had been no evidence of poison in his stomach, or bruises, abrasions, or wounds upon his body, and that there could be no doubt but that death had been the result of an attack of acute endocarditis.

The jury was out but fifteen minutes, returning a verdict of not guilty on the first ballot. To June Lathrop it meant nothing. It was what she had expected; but though it freed her from an unjust charge, it could never right the hideous wrong that had been done her, first by an individual in conceiving and perpetrating the wrong, and then by the community, as represented by the police, in dragging the whole hideous fabric of her shame before the world.

As is customary upon the acquittal of a defendant in a criminal case, a horde of the morbidly curious thronged about June to offer their congratulations. She turned from them wearily, seeking her mother; but there was one who would not be denied — a tall, freckled youth who wormed his way to her side with uncanny stealthiness. It was Sammy, the one-time office-boy of the corporation known as John Secor & Co.

"Miss Lathrop," he whispered. "Miss Lathrop, I've been trying to find you for years. I'm a regular detective now; but the best job I ever did I did for you and nobody never knew anything about it. Don't you remember me?"

She shook hands with him, and he followed her from the court-room. There was another who followed her, too. A sun-tanned young man whose haggard features bore clear witness to the mental suffering he had endured.

Outside the building he touched her sleeve. She turned toward him.

"Do you loathe me," he whispered, "for what *he* did?"

"You know better than that," she answered; "but now you see why it was that I could not marry you. Now you will thank me for not being weak and giving in — God knows how sorely I was tempted!"

"There is nothing now to prevent," he said eagerly.

She looked at him in surprise. "You still want me?" she cried. "You can't mean it — it would be horrible!"

"I shall always want you, June," he said doggedly, "and some day I shall have you."

But still she shook her head.

"It would be wicked, Ogden," she said with a little

shudder. "If he had been any one else — any one else in the world than your father!"

Secor looked at her in astonishment.

"My father!" he exclaimed. "Do you mean that you do not know — that John Secor was *not* my father?"

The girl's astonishment and incredulity were writ plain upon her face.

"Not your father?" It was scarce a whisper.

"I was the foster son of John Secor's brother. When he died I went to live with the John Secors, and after the death of their only son I entered Mr. Secor's office, taking the place of the son he had lost, later inheriting his business."

June continued to look in dull bewilderment at Secor. It could not be true! She cast about for another obstacle. Certainly she had no right to such happiness as she saw being surely pressed upon her.

"There is still the charge against me of having aided the men who robbed your safe — that is even worse, for it reproaches me with disloyalty and treachery toward one who had befriended me," she said faintly.

Sammy and June's mother had been standing a little apart as the two spoke together in whispers. June had slightly raised her voice as she recalled the affair in the office of John Secor & Co. the night that Ogden had received the blows that had resulted in all his financial troubles.

That part Sammy heard. Now he stepped forward.

"That's what I wanted to tell you about, Miss Lathrop," he said, excitedly. "It wasn't her at all" he went on, turning toward Secor. "It was that smooth scoundrel of a Stickler. I was hiding under his filing cabinet when he tried to make Miss Lathrop go out with him, and I heard her turn him down. Then I followed him, for I was just studying to be a detective then and I had to practice every chance I got. He went straight to Abe Farris's saloon, and there I saw him talking low and confidential-like to a couple of tough-lookin' guys for about two hours. He handed one of 'em a slip of paper, explaining what was on it. I couldn't see it, but from what happened after I knew it held the combination to your safe, for I seen the robber that was shot when he was put on trial, and he was one of the guys that Stickler met in Farris's. I was so scared I didn't dare tell nobody."

Ogden turned toward June with a faint smile. "You see," he said, "that one by one your defenses are re-duced — aren't you about ready to capitulate?"

"I guess there is no other way," she sighed; "but it seems that the world must be all awry when hope of happiness appears so close within my grasp!"

Printed in the United States
16123LVS00001B/76-81